SECOND CHANCES

AMANDA RADLEY

SIGN UP TO WIN

Firstly, thank you for purchasing *Second Chances* I really appreciate your support and hope you enjoy the book!

Head over to my website and sign up to my mailing list to be kept up to date with all my latest releases, promotions, and giveaways.

www.amandaradley.com

SECOND CHANCES

FIRST DAY OF SCHOOL

Preparations for the first day of school were as hectic as Hannah expected them to be. At twenty-five years old, she had hoped that she would be a little better organised, not flitting around the cramped apartment like she was attached to a bungee rope.

It would have been a little more acceptable if it had been *her* first day of school.

"Are you nearly ready, Mummy?" Rosie asked patiently.

Hannah stopped in the middle of the apartment, her hands full of dirty laundry and the paperwork she'd just discovered under the plant on the dining table. She looked at Rosie and smiled.

Her daughter was dressed in her uniform, previously seen only once before in the shop it was bought in. Although, if Rosie had her way, she'd have worn it every day throughout July and August, such was her excitement about finally starting school.

Her hair was neatly brushed, the school-approved

headband in forest green and black firmly in place on top of her head. The green cardigan was a size too big, her fingers just visible through the ends of the sleeves. The dark grey skirt only fitted after a couple of rolls of the elasticated waistband.

The oversized uniform was not down to Hannah purchasing a larger size for Rosie to grow into, although she completely understood the parents who did this. Uniforms were expensive, and children grew quickly, especially when they were five years old. The excess material was simply because Rosie was small for her age, having not yet had a growth spurt. Hannah had purchased the smallest size available, but the clothes still swamped Rosie.

Not that she said anything. Rosie was so proud to be in a uniform, and Hannah didn't want to dampen her spirits by admitting that she looked like five pounds of potatoes in a ten-pound sack.

Hannah wasn't too worried. She was five-foot-eight herself and assumed that Rosie would eventually catch up. She hoped it would be sooner rather than later. Rosie already looked a little out of place in comparison to the children she played with. It was quite noticeable when she attended a friend's birthday party, or when she joined other children in the playground of the local park.

Hannah didn't want Rosie to look out of place on her first day of school. She knew that first impressions mattered. Growing up in a small town like Fairlight meant that Rosie would be stuck with her classmates for the rest of her school career. Potentially the rest of her life, if she followed in her mother's regrettable footsteps and decided to stay on in her hometown.

"Mummy?" Rosie asked again, fidgeting a bit with her sleeves.

Hannah looked at the clock on the wall. Ten minutes until they had to leave. She threw the laundry and the papers onto the sofa. They could be dealt with later.

"We need to get you some breakfast, pumpkin," Hannah said, already mentally calculating what could be prepared in two minutes and eaten on the move.

"I already had breakfast," Rosie replied.

Hannah came to a dead stop. She looked from her daughter to the kitchen, noticing Rosie's step stool in front of the sink and a washed bowl standing up on the silver dish drainer.

"What did you have?" Hannah asked. She opened a cupboard door and grabbed a cereal bar for herself. "And when?"

"When you were in the shower. I had Frosted Flakes. They are tasty, but I think there's too much sugar in them."

"There is," Hannah agreed. "Maybe we should get you something else for the future?"

"Yes, please."

Hannah pulled out the breadboard and reached for the packet of bread on the countertop.

"I made my lunch," Rosie added.

Hannah paused. She shouldn't have been surprised. Rosie had been practically self-sufficient since the moment she could walk. She'd quickly gone from helping her mother with meals to making basic ones by herself.

Hannah knew that many parents would be happy for

the help around the house, and she was. But it also made her feel redundant.

It was Rosie's first day of school, and like most children on Christmas morning, she had awoken early. Unlike most children, she had gotten herself ready for school without any assistance from her mother. She'd gotten dressed, brushed her hair, eaten breakfast, and made her own packed lunch.

Hannah felt guilty. She wanted to do those things for Rosie, but the knowledge that her only daughter was leaving the nest for full-time school had created a whirlwind of panic and protectiveness which had swirled inside her for the last few months. That panic had culminated in a near meltdown that morning.

While Rosie was no doubt methodically buttering bread for a sandwich, Hannah had been nearing a panic attack while she showered. Memories of her own time at school had haunted her the previous night.

She put away the breadboard and the bread and took a deep breath to remind herself that everything was going to be fine. She turned around and regarded Rosie again.

"I'll make your lunch tomorrow," she said.

"I don't mind," Rosie replied.

"I know you don't mind," Hannah said as she knelt to Rosie's level, "but I'm your mother and it's my job. You wouldn't want to take my job and make me unemployed, would you?"

Rosie giggled. "That's silly."

"Oh, is it?" Hannah grinned. "I bet you're the only person starting school today who made their own breakfast *and* lunch. All those other mummies and daddies are working hard, but I'm just stood here." She shrugged her shoulders. "Nothing to do. I bet you even packed your bag."

Rosie pointed to the rucksack by the front door.

Hannah looked at it and sighed, the flaky paint on the doorframe reminding her that she needed to find some time to decorate.

"It's okay, Mummy," Rosie said. "I like doing things."

"I know you do, pumpkin. Don't worry, I'm just being silly. I'm going to miss you."

Rosie giggled again. "It's only until three o'clock."

"That's a lot of hours," Hannah said playfully. "I think it's about a hundred and seventy-two hours."

Rosie burst out laughing. "No, it isn't!"

"Oh, isn't it? That's good." Hannah picked up the cereal bar and threw it into her shoulder bag. She looked through the messy contents to check she had everything she'd need for work. Satisfied, she shouldered the bag and grabbed Rosie's coat from the rack.

"Do I look okay?" her daughter asked. She lifted her arms a little and did a small, shy twirl.

"You look perfect, pumpkin," Hannah reassured her. She didn't elaborate. She guessed that Rosie had realised her clothes didn't quite fit, and she didn't want to worry her. "You look just like someone who is having their very... first... day... of... school!" she said excitedly, knowing that Rosie was full to bursting with anticipation.

The beam that spread across Rosie's face nearly made the dread in the pit of Hannah's stomach vanish.

Nearly.

"And remember that Daniel and Simone will be there,

so you already have two friends," Hannah said, putting her own coat on.

"I know." Rosie picked up her bag. "They went to Reception though, so they probably know some of the others."

Hannah's heart sank. The optional part-time introduction to primary school, known as Reception classes, were just not feasible with her working hours and the cost of a babysitter to take Rosie to and from Reception in the middle of the day. It had been a difficult decision not to enrol Rosie in Reception, but there had been no other option at the time.

"Then they can introduce you," Hannah said, even though she knew it wouldn't be the same. Five-year-olds didn't cordially introduce their friends to their other friends. Rosie had definitely missed out on opportunities to make some friends by not attending part-time school. Hannah had to hope that she'd connect with some of her classmates regardless.

"Anyway, we better get going," she said, not wanting to dwell too long on the possibility that her lack of finances had socially crippled her daughter before she'd even stepped through the school gates.

They exited the apartment and walked down the narrow corridor of steps to street level. They lived above the village post office, which meant accessing their home via a doorway next to the busy shop and climbing a steep set of stairs.

It wasn't ideal. The community of Fairlight was not known for their discretion. A single mother living just above the poverty line in the run-down apartment above a busy community hub was like catnip for many residents.

Hannah unlocked the street door and gestured for Rosie to exit into the September sunlight. As she locked up behind her, she heard Mrs Simmons telling Rosie that she looked lovely in her new uniform and wishing well for her first day.

She turned around, and Mrs Simmons quickly averted her eyes. The old busybody dashed into the post office, clearly keen to avoid communicating with her. Hannah was used to it. She'd grown up in Fairlight as an outcast and didn't expect anything else. She was grateful that everyone treated Rosie with kindness and respect, even if that didn't extend to herself. She was an adult who could deal with the looks and the whispers.

Rosie reached up and clutched her hand. They walked past the small row of shops, toward Willows School.

"What do you think my teacher will be like?" Rosie asked.

"Hairy," Hannah said. "With big teeth."

"It's a woman," Rosie pointed out. "Her name is Miss Spencer."

Hannah didn't recognise the name. *Miss Spencer must be new, then, poor thing,* she thought. "Then she'll be *very* hairy with *enormous* teeth," Hannah corrected herself. "And a big eye in the back of her head."

"I think she will be very nice," Rosie said, ignoring her mother's silly comments.

"She'll be very nice to you, pumpkin," Hannah issued a promise she hoped would be true.

They joined the sparse stream of other parents walking

their children to the school. Hannah nodded her greetings to the ones she recognised, and Rosie offered shy waves to children.

The road swept downward toward the cliffs, which were the visual highlight of the otherwise lacklustre town. The waves of the English Channel could be heard crashing against the rocks below. The choppy water had come into view, and Hannah stared at the expanse of dark blue, knowing that autumn's limited visibility was on the way.

Willows School was situated near the end of the coastal road in a Victorian building, which hadn't changed much since it was built. Every step Hannah took felt slightly heavier than the one which preceded it. She remembered the dread of attending the school, hating every single day with a passion. Back then, she never thought she'd see a day where she would be leading her own flesh and blood down the bleak path toward a building which looked eerily like a prison.

"Do you think we'll get homework?" Rosie asked, excitement evident in her tone.

"Maybe," Hannah replied. "You'll have to ask."

She knew Rosie wouldn't ask. Not yet, anyway. As chatty as Rosie was with her, she was very shy and introverted with new people. She doubted her eagerness at beginning school would overcome her nerves on the first day, or even in the first week.

She hoped Rosie would make some friends quickly, though, and that that would enable her to come out of her shell. But she also wondered if she needed to come out of her shell in order to make friends.

Hannah's heart thudded against her ribcage. She

wanted to scoop Rosie into a hug and take her home, protecting her from the terrible social rituals that were built into school life, but she knew that wouldn't help Rosie in the slightest.

Hannah's biggest fear was that Rosie would be treated as she had been at school. Ostracised and bullied. Sticking out, being different, had been Hannah's downfall. She knew she could prevent that for Rosie. She could help her to fit in, and that would lead to friends.

"Will you pick me up from school or will Uncle Adrian?" Rosie asked.

"I'll be picking you up, and I have something special planned."

Rosie looked up at her, big brown eyes wide and questioning.

"But it's a surprise," Hannah added.

Rosie's hand tightened around hers. "This is going to be the best day ever."

Hannah smiled. Only her daughter would say that about the first day of school.

2

WELCOME TO WILLOWS

"THIS WILL BE your form room, Miss Spencer." Mr Hardaker held the door opened and gestured for Alice to step inside.

"Thank you, headmaster." She stepped around the elderly man and into the room.

She was immediately struck by how lifeless and cold it seemed. The entire school building was, of course, dated, but this room in particular seemed to have been left to languish decades ago.

Many schools in Britain were located in buildings which had been built over a hundred years ago. Willows Primary School was one such building and was in complete contrast to Alice's previous employment in a modern inner-city school in Manchester.

She looked around the room, taking in the high ceilings and the large, single-glazed windows. The floor built of faded wooden planks seemingly held together by an accumulation of lacquer which had been applied over the years.

There was still an old-fashioned chalkboard along one wall, though another wall had a more modern whiteboard. The furniture was old and worn, still serviceable but nothing like the new desks and chairs she was used to.

In many ways, Willows reminded her of the schools from her youth and bore little resemblance to any of the schools she had taught at during her career.

"If you need anything, then it will probably be best to speak with Miss Gibson. She knows more than I do," Mr Hardaker said. "I'll leave you to prepare for your lesson."

He turned and shuffled away before she had a chance to say anything else.

Alice let out a breath and slowly circled the room to explore her new surroundings. The form room was on the first floor of the building and allowed for magnificent views of the cliffs and the English Channel in the distance. She took a small step back, her fear of heights quietly suggesting that the windows in such an old building were not as stable as they seemed.

"It's a great view, but the kids do find it distracting. Especially when there's a tanker tooting away."

Alice turned around. A short, curvy woman with a blonde bob had entered the room. She hugged a bunch of folders and papers to her chest.

"I'm Lucy Gibson, general go-to person. You must be Alice Spencer?"

"I am."

"Welcome to Willows. The building is falling down and Hardaker doesn't know what day of the week it is, but most of the kids are okay and the village can be quite picturesque in summer," Lucy said.

"Shame I've arrived in September," Alice quipped.

"Yes," Lucy chuckled. "It will be pretty much fog and terrible weather now until at least next June. What brings you to Fairlight, if I may ask? Obviously feel free to fudge the truth if you're in witness protection."

Alice smiled. She'd yet to meet anyone in Fairlight aside from her landlord. She had a feeling she'd get on well with Lucy.

"I fancied a change of pace, smaller class sizes, and the opportunity to actually get to know the children," she explained. There was a little more to it than that, but it would do for a start.

"You'll get all of that here. You were up in Manchester, weren't you?" Lucy asked. It was obvious she already knew her work history.

"I was, right in the city. Very big, very busy school. I enjoyed it and had a lot of opportunities to teach different years, but I wanted something different."

"And you heard about Fairlight, got your map and a magnifying glass out, and thought you'd come here?" Lucy joked.

It wasn't far off the truth. When the recruitment consultant had mentioned Fairlight, she'd had no idea where it was. It had taken a Google Maps search and few clicks on the plus symbol before she found the small costal village.

"Isn't that how all relocation decisions are made?" she replied with a grin.

"I wouldn't know, I've lived here my entire life. I admire your courage to up and move yourself down here."

"I'm not sure how courageous it was," Alice confessed.

"You can tell me all about it after school one day," Lucy said. "I don't want to sound like we're stuck in a horror movie, but we don't get many new people in town. I'm happy to be your guide, so if you need anything either here at Willows or in general, just let me know. I'm three doors up." She nodded toward the corridor.

"Thank you, that's really kind of you. I'll definitely take you up on that." Alice had only been in Fairlight a few days, one for the initial interview three months ago, and two since she had moved. Already she was keenly aware of the close-knit community. She'd need to make an effort to settle in or else she would stick out. In Manchester, there were so many people that you were left to get on with things. Fairlight, on the other hand, seemed to be the kind of place where everyone would know their neighbours.

"Now, for the bad news," Lucy continued. "You're on duty at morning break in playground with me."

All teachers loathed being on playground duty, no matter what. Standing around outside minding the children was never any fun. There were always troublemakers, bullies, scuffles, misunderstandings, tears, and tantrums. However, it came with the territory of being a teacher, and Alice knew to take it in her stride. Besides, it would help her to learn more about the children who attended Willows.

"I quit, I'm heading back to Manchester," she joked.

"Too late, we have you now!" Lucy winked. She turned on her heel and left the room.

Alice smiled to herself. After meeting Hardaker, it was

a relief to know that at least one of her co-workers was under seventy and had a sense of humour.

She looked at her watch and realised that lessons would be starting shortly. She needed to prepare to welcome her new students not just to their new form room and to herself, but also to school as a whole.

After sixteen years of teaching all ages, she'd decided to stick to teaching year one, the five- and six-year-olds just starting their official education. To her, they were the most rewarding to teach. Many of her ex-colleagues would disagree. She'd received many commiserating back pats when she told them she was leaving to teach year one in a pinprick of a village on the South Coast.

The desks were lined up in regimental rows, definitely not very welcoming or conducive to helping younger children to relax. She pulled the chairs out and rearranged the tables, pushing them together to make larger ones where children would be made to sit together rather than all alone.

She made two large tables and placed six chairs around each of them in a horseshoe shape to face the front of the classroom. Twelve students was a lot fewer than the twenty-nine she was used to.

She stood back and looked at the room, letting out a frustrated sigh as she did. The walls were bland, the stereotypical white-painted brickwork seen in so many similar buildings. Clearly all of the schoolwork from the previous year had been disposed of or given back to the children at the end of the term. Now she was left with what might generously be described as a blank canvas. Sadly, the canvas was chipped, stained, and stark, highlighting an already cold and inhospitable feel.

She made a mental note to speak with Lucy about any possible redecorating budget. Even a standard whitewash would make it look less like it had been abandoned fifty years ago.

She could hear the sounds of children playing and decided it was time to head out to the playground to welcome her new intake. She pulled her coat tight around her, only now realising she hadn't taken it off. She hoped the cold air in the building was simply due a lack of heating during the holidays. A glance at the old iron radiator in the corner had her wondering just how well the heating worked.

"Make the best of it," she mumbled to herself. "Give it a year."

3

RETURN TO THE SCHOOL GATES

THE CLOSER THEY got to the gates, the more the anxiety bubbled up inside Hannah and the more excited Rosie became. Looking at the building, Hannah couldn't believe how literally nothing had changed since her own time there. The school still towered over her, the iron gates were still coated in peeling, dark green paint.

She gripped Rosie's hand a little tighter, partly due to the memories starting to creep from the dark recesses of her mind and partly because she didn't want to leave Rosie for an entire school day.

"There's Simone!" Rosie pointed into the playground and tugged on Hannah's hand with excitement.

"Off you go." Hannah let go. Though she would spend this first day apart missing her little girl, she was happy that Rosie was as excited about socialising with a real person as she often was about getting a new book.

Rosie hurried off. Hannah had to smother a smirk behind her hand. The rucksack on her back was laden with all the so-called essentials Rosie thought she might need. Sadly, the bulk of the bag meant that her top speed had been severely reduced. She waddled like a tortoise who had just learnt to stand up right.

Hannah stepped across the threshold of the gate. A shiver ran down her spine. She saw some parents she knew from the park and walked over to join them. It would have been preferable to leave, but she knew she should wait for the morning bell indicating the start of the school day to see Rosie safely inside. Even if her fight-or-flight responses were definitely screaming flight.

"Morning," she greeted the others, shoving her hands into her pockets and looking at the children playing rather than the group she had joined.

A murmur of greetings followed.

"As I said, Peter is so nervous about starting school," Nadine, one of the mums, said.

"So's Simone," Sue replied. "She's excited, too, but she couldn't sleep last night."

"Same," another mum chipped in. "I was awake all night wondering if there was anything I'd forgotten. Wondering if I'd ironed the school uniform and bought the right pens and pencils."

"Same, I didn't sleep a wink," Nadine said. "Have any of you met this Miss Spencer?"

"No, I just know that she's new," Sue replied. "From Manchester, apparently."

"What's she doing down here?" Nadine asked. "Seems like a step backwards to me."

"Seems very odd," a father in the group agreed.

Hannah rolled her eyes. This was one of the things she hated about Fairlight: the gossip. Everyone was so starved for someone to chat about that the moment someone new appeared, they pounced.

Although, she had to admit that she was also curious about the newcomer. Whoever she was, she'd be looking after Rosie every weekday for the next year.

"Couldn't find anything on Facebook," Nadine said.

"I looked on LinkedIn," Sue replied, smugly. "Couldn't see much, though, just a photograph."

Hannah dug her hands deeper into her coat pockets and started to clench and unclench her fists. These people were unbelievable. Time and access to the Internet had made them worse over the years. It didn't help that Hannah knew she had often been the subject of similar chattering circles. She wondered how much dirt they had dug up on her and spread around Fairlight without her knowledge.

"In fact, there she is," Sue said.

Hannah looked up, seeing Sue gesture with her chin towards the main entrance to the building. She turned and felt her eyes start to widen. Miss Spencer was gorgeous. A little older than she'd expected, possibly late thirties, shoulder-length, dark brown hair. She wore a long, black coat, and Hannah itched to know what was beneath. She could see knee-high boots which indicated a skirt.

If I had a teacher like that, I might have paid more attention, Hannah thought to herself. *Although probably not to the schoolwork.*

Miss Spencer walked into the playground and spoke to a group of children standing nearest the door. The children animatedly spoke with her.

"At least she's younger than Hardaker," Nadine said.

"It's hard to find anyone older than Hardaker," Sue replied.

Their voices faded into the background as Hannah watched Miss Spencer interacting with the children. She couldn't hear what was being said, but the children were obviously having a lot of fun. Their laughter could be heard across the playground.

Hannah found herself getting lost in Miss Spencer's smile.

"Hannah?"

She turned around. "Hm?"

"I asked if Rosie attended Reception," Nadine said.

Hannah dampened down the deep breath she wanted to take. Nadine knew that Rosie hadn't attended. What she wanted to ask was, why hadn't she? Hannah wasn't about to answer that question.

"No, she didn't," Hannah said, turning her attention back to the children playing.

"Oh, shame. I know Peter benefitted from seeing the school and getting to know some of the structure and routine. But I'm sure Rosie will fit in just fine," Nadine said.

"I'm sure she will," Hannah agreed.

She wasn't about to explain her work situation and justify her decisions to Nadine. She'd learnt long ago that the best way to not be part of the gossip circle was to not feed them any new information.

A loud bell rang from the school's clock tower.

Rosie turned around from where she was talking to Simone and waved happily at Hannah. She waved back, a part of her relieved that Rosie wasn't going to come over and hug her. She had a suspicion that if she did, she'd wrap her arms around her daughter and take her back home. Everyone had always told her that children grew up fast, but she hadn't expected it to be so true.

It felt like only a year ago that Rosie was a baby. Now here she was, five years old, and about to start her first day at school. Hannah's gaze turned to Miss Spencer. She was assisting some of the other teachers in getting the children in from the playground. Hannah grinned. There were always some kids who would sprint around like Usain Bolt one last time before being confined to a desk for six hours. She couldn't blame them.

Even so, she couldn't take her eyes off Miss Spencer.

"Will we see you at the coffee morning on Wednesday?" Sue asked, rudely stopping in front of her line of vision.

"No, sorry, I can't," Hannah murmured. "Working."

She wasn't at all sorry. She couldn't think of anything worse than spending a whole morning with these people. She could just imagine the gossiping and the lying that went on. She remembered when everyone turned on Nigel Garfield because he got a new car. The rumour was that he was on state benefits and didn't work because no one saw him leave his house. When the new car turned up, there was a silent uproar. He was a benefits cheat, and everyone was talking about it. Behind Nigel's back, of course.

Three months later, Hannah saw Nigel in the supermarket and asked him what he did for a living. Turned out he was an accountant who worked from home. Mystery solved.

But for three months he was, unknowingly, the subject on everyone's lips.

Hannah knew all too well that her avoidance meant that she was probably a topic of conversation. She knew for certain that she had been in the past.

"Oh, well, let us know if you get some time off. We'd love to see you there," Sue replied.

"Sure. See you later." Hannah turned and walked away from the parents at a quick pace. She had no interest in walking back to town with anyone else. Every time someone spoke to her, she felt for sure that they were seeking out more fuel for the conversational fire. Things to report back to the others on.

Her dad told her she was paranoid, but he didn't really know. He may have lived in Fairlight years ago, but his work kept him away for so long that he never really got to know the residents like she had. And now he was about as far away from Fairlight as he could get, living in Scotland. She often wondered if she should have followed him.

Often wondered why she hadn't.

The walk to Chopz Hairdressing Salon flew by, especially because Hannah was moving at a brisk pace to ensure the other parents didn't catch up.

She opened the door, the bell tinkling as she did.

Adrian poked his head out from the back room in case she was a client.

"Just me," she greeted.

"How did it go?" He stepped into the salon and regarded her sadly.

"Heartbreaking," she admitted. "But I have to accept that she is growing up."

"Where does the time go?" he asked.

"I don't know, but I'd like some of it back." She took off her coat and walked to the back of the room to hang it in the closet.

The phone rang. Adrian answered in his usual vibrant manner. She hoped it was one of her clients making an appointment. It was early on in the month, but her pay packet was already looking a little light.

It was to be expected at that time of year. Summer was dwindling, Christmas was miles away. The time between haircutting appointments started to increase, and, with it, Hannah's salary decreased.

She'd been styling hair long enough to expect the drop in wages at this time of year, but she still found herself on edge. She dreamed of a time when she would be able to get through a month without relying on the money her father sent. She told him not to bother, he was a pensioner and needed to save his money. But every month an amount would arrive, accompanied by a text explaining that the money was for Rosie.

Of course, she was grateful for the funds. Most of the time she needed them, not that she'd ever admit that to him. She wished she didn't need to rely on money from her father. It was another nail in the coffin of her self-confidence.

Adrian hung up the phone. "Mrs Philips wants to see you tomorrow. I think she wants that colour done again." He raised his eyebrows and shook his head.

Hannah rolled her eyes. "How do you nicely tell a seventy-year-old to not dye their hair raven black? I think I've tried every subtle way I can think of."

"It's extra money," Adrian pointed out.

"Which I'm grateful for, but it's hardly a good advertising board to have walking around the village," Hannah pointed out.

"True. Have another word with her, see if you can tame it down. Tell her that all the old biddies are going light lilac these days."

"I'll use those exact words." Hannah winked.

She walked into the staff room and made herself a cup of tea. She was in desperate need of the cereal bar she had thrown in her bag that morning.

Adrian entered the room and looked at the boiling kettle. "Yes, please."

Hannah got another mug out of the cupboard.

"Will you be able to go up to London on the twenty-ninth?" he asked. "There's a course for that new range of gels and waxes the rep has been trying to sell us for the last three months. I'm thinking of taking a few and then getting some money off the course."

Hannah smiled to herself as she made the tea. Adrian was always helping her keep her training up to date. Of course, he pretended it was because he couldn't be bothered going himself, but she knew that he was really doing it to help her career and make her the best stylist she could be.

"Depends on the times," she admitted. "I'd need to be back in time to pick Rosie up from school."

"I think it's in the morning, so you should get back in time. If not, then I'll go and pick her up," he offered.

"Is there really a course, or do you just want to spend more time with your favourite person?" Hannah joked.

He pulled out a chair and sat down. "You got me. I just want you out of the way so we can get some more colouring in done."

"You know Rosie hasn't really enjoyed colouring in for about a year. She's just doing it because you like it," Hannah told him.

"And that's why I like spending time with her. She's kind and thoughtful, unlike her mother."

Hannah turned and smiled sweetly at him. "Remind me how much crushed glass you want in your tea?"

"Just the usual two spoons."

She made the tea, placed the two mugs on the table, and sat down. Her eyes drifted to the third chair at the table. Rosie spent so much time in the staff room at the salon that she had her own dedicated seat. Seeing it made Hannah miss Rosie and wonder how her first day was going.

"She'll be fine," Adrian said, seemingly reading her mind.

"I know, I know. I can't help but worry." She sipped her tea. "My time at school wasn't exactly blissful."

"Yeah, but your hair was terrible, so you were asking for it," Adrian said in an attempt to make light of the deep emotional scars which he knew Hannah suffered.

"True," she agreed. "I needed a perm, like you."

"My hair is naturally curly," Adrian argued with a grin. "But, back to the point, Rosie will be fine."

"She's so shy, I worry she won't speak to anyone. She only really speaks to you, me, and two of her friends. What if she doesn't say anything?"

"She'll speak eventually," Adrian reassured her. "And

when she does, everyone will love her. She's so bright, she'll be running the place by the end of the week."

Panic raced through Hannah. She shook her head. "I hope not. I want her to have a normal school experience. Make friends, get good grades, the end."

Adrian looked at her sceptically.

"What?" she asked.

"You know that's not likely to happen. Well, the good grades bit will most definitely happen. But a normal school experience? Doubtful. Rosie is special."

Hannah sagged forward. It was the last thing she wanted to hear. She'd spent weeks convincing herself that Rosie would have a normal, happy school life. Not stand out from the crowd.

"I just want her to be happy," Hannah said softly.

"She will be. She'll be prime minister when she grows up. Of the world." Adrian nodded emphatically.

Hannah put her head in her hands. She didn't want to hold Rosie back, but she also didn't want her to be treated differently because of her abilities, especially in the first year of school. Maybe she'd be ready for Rosie to shine in a few more years, but right now, she wanted her little girl to blend in and remain a happy little girl.

"Hey, don't worry. It will all be fine," Adrian said.

She sat up and offered him a smile before taking a sip of her tea. She didn't believe that for a second.

4

FIRST IMPRESSIONS

THE CHILDREN SETTLED QUICKLY, and Alice stood in front of the class. Twelve eager but nervous faces stared back at her.

"Good morning, class," she said.

Three quarters of the children replied with a singsong "Good morning, Miss Spencer." The remaining children looked confused.

"I can see that some of you have attended Reception classes," Alice said. "For those of you who didn't, when I say good morning to you, you say good morning to me. Shall we try that again?" A flurry of agreeing nods met her. "Good morning, class."

"Good morning, Miss Spencer!" all of the children greeted her loudly.

She took a step back and laughed, covering her ears. "That was very good, class, but I think we should tone it down just a little in the future. Otherwise we might get complaints from the other students."

She walked over to her desk and picked up a marker pen.

"Now, I want to welcome you all to year one, and my class. I know some of you have been to Reception, but this year will be a little different."

Less painting with potatoes and playing snakes and ladders, she told herself.

"Firstly, I'm your form tutor. You are welcome to talk to me about anything. If you need anything, if you're worried about anything, I'm always here for you. If you can't find me, then you can always speak to one of the other teachers. No question is silly or wrong. We're here to help you. Does that make sense?"

She held the children's gaze until the nods came, wanting to ensure that they all understood. She knew that the first day of school was daunting, and she was about to launch into the rules of school which were enough to leave any child shell-shocked.

She pulled the lid from the marker pen and approached the whiteboard.

"Now, because there are a lot of us, it's important that we make some rules to ensure that everything runs smoothly in the classroom. Can anyone think of some rules that we should put on the whiteboard?"

A boy called—she checked her roster—James thrust his hand into the air.

Alice gestured to him. "Yes, James?"

"Be nice!" James shouted.

"That's a very good idea, James," she said. She wrote the words on the whiteboard. "But can you think of examples of that? What kinds of things can we do to be nice?"

"Say 'thank you'!" a girl named Simone called out.

"That's a great suggestion, Simone," she said, "but when you have something to say, you need to remember to put your hand up and answer when I call on you, okay? Just in case there are lots of people who have suggestions. Does that make sense?"

"Yes, Miss Spencer," Simone replied happily.

She carried on questioning the children about what rules they should have for the next thirty minutes. All the usual suspects came up. Saying please, thank you, and excuse me. Putting your hand up to answer questions. No shouting. No running. Be polite. Do as you are asked to do, right away.

Alice enjoyed making rules with the class. In their hearts, the children already knew what they should and should not be doing. In reality, it was made up of behaviours they already understood, but by getting the children to make the list, she ensured that they felt like they were making, setting, and adhering to their own rules, not the rules of a stuck-in-the-mud teacher.

It was also a very quick way to find out the troublemakers, those who thought any suggestion would make it onto the board, like all-day playtime and going home early. Colin was one such troublemaker whom she'd already made a mental note to keep an eye on.

One of her key jobs early on in meeting the new intakes was to figure out their personalities and levels of education. At such a young age, the differences in children in the same class could be startling.

"So, what does everyone think about the form room?" Alice asked, gesturing around the empty space. Before they had a chance to answer she made a face. "It's a bit boring, isn't it?"

The children looked around the room and nodded.

"Don't worry, we'll have this room bursting with fun and colour in no time at all," she reassured them. "Because we'll be putting some of your work on the walls. Won't that be exciting?"

"My mummy says we can't draw on the walls," James said.

"And she's right," Alice agreed. "But we can put pieces of paper on the walls. If we're working on a special project, then we can use it to decorate. Once it's been marked, of course."

James looked thoughtful. She hoped she hadn't caused his mother any problems.

The chatty girl next to James, Sarah, started to tell him about all the things she put on her bedroom wall at home. Clearly, Sarah's mum wasn't as concerned about the state of her walls.

As the children started to chip in on the subject, Alice glanced at the rest of the class, already feeling as if she had a good idea about most of them. One, however, had remained very quiet. She crossed over to her desk and glanced at the register, quickly finding the name of the silent student.

Rose Hall.

She wasn't about to push Rose too much on her first day, but she made a mental note to keep an eye on her. Most shy children would start to speak after a day or two. Some of the noisiest children she had taught had initially been very quiet.

She looked at her watch and noted that ten o'clock was fast approaching.

"Class, class," she said to get their attention.

They quickly quietened down.

"It's nearly time for break, so I think it would be a good idea if we started to get our coats on. It's a little chilly today."

She'd barely finished speaking before the sound of chairs scraping on the wooden floor filled the room. One wall had a row of clothes pegs where an assortment of coats were hung. Alice regarded them, wondering how much effort it would be to put name cards above them and maybe a small storage box below, so the children had somewhere for scarves and gloves.

James was circling himself, trying to put his arm in his jacket. Alice quickly stepped forward and held the coat steady for him.

"Thank you," he said. He turned around and looked up at her expectantly.

She crouched down and took his hands in hers, guiding his small fingers to the buttons. As she helped him to do his coat up, she looked at the other children. Many were struggling to either put their coats on or do them up.

School was often one of the first experiences where children had to fend for themselves with certain aspects of life. At home, a parent may be so keen to hurry up and get out of the house that they assisted the child with basic tasks, which meant that the children often struggled to perform those tasks on their own.

It was a stark reminder how young the children were, despite starting full-time education, and that it was her job to make the transition from child to student as seamless as possible.

She finished helping James with his coat and found that a line had formed behind him. Sarah was next, needing assistance with her zip.

"Zips are tricky," Alice reassured her upon noticing embarrassed eyes.

She looked up and saw that Rose had her coat on, zipped up, and was putting on her gloves.

"I don't like zips," Sarah said. "I got my finger stuck and it bleeded."

"It bled," Alice corrected. "I've done that, too, it can be quite painful. You need to keep your fingers out of the way and then you'll not have any problems."

She did the zip up and smiled at Sarah.

"Thank you, miss," Sarah answered and hurried away before the next child stepped up.

Alice decided she'd give them all this first week. After that they would have to be able to get themselves ready alone. It was hard because she wanted to help, but she knew she wasn't really helping them if she didn't make them independent.

It was a fine balance, one she had to get right.

Alice stood in the playground, watching the children. There were considerably fewer here than she was used to. At her previous schools, there had been hundreds, sometimes even over a thousand students. But Willows was a small school serving a few local villages, and she estimated there were only around sixty children in total.

That didn't make playtime any less daunting.

Like water spilt from a glass, the children were everywhere and potentially getting themselves into trouble. Some were running, some were on the old play equipment which had seen better days. Some were sitting on the grass in groups, and some were alone.

Keeping an adequate eye on all of them was a difficult task, especially when she was surrounded by some members of the new intake who found the playground overwhelming.

"Sarah, why don't you go and play with Simone?" Alice suggested kindly. While she was happy that Sarah felt comfortable around her, she couldn't be her safety blanket forever. The sooner the children learnt to mix and mingle, the better all around.

Sarah looked into the distance where Simone was swinging from the monkey bars.

"Maybe," she said thoughtfully.

"Thomas Lassiter!" Alice turned to see her co-worker Lucy Gibson bellowing from the school entrance, having just arrived for playground duty. "Get down!"

Alice followed Lucy's gaze to a boy climbing the perimeter fence. She wanted to kick herself for not noticing.

Reluctantly, Thomas jumped down. "Sorry, Miss Gibson."

Lucy joined Alice. She pulled on her gloves and looked around the playground with an eagle eye.

"Sorry, I didn't even notice that," Alice apologised.

"No problem, he literally just jumped up," Lucy explained. "You can't have eyes in the back of your head here."

The approach of the shouty teacher caused Alice's group of nervous students to take their chances with the playground.

"There were so many more of us on duty in my old school," Alice explained.

"You'll get used to it," Lucy reassured her, her eyes sweeping around the playground as she spoke.

Alice got the impression that Lucy was one of those teachers that even the naughtiest of children refused to mess with. Her volume was as impressive as her ability to notice the tiniest details.

"How's things with your new class?" Lucy asked.

"Good." Alice looked over the children, seeking out her own. "I've had a little pushback from a couple, but most are settling in well."

"There's always one or two who want to test your limits," Lucy agreed.

"That's true. Hopefully, we'll iron that out quickly. On another note, I wanted to ask, what are my chances of getting some money to decorate my form room?" Alice asked.

Lucy snorted a laugh. "Absolute zero, I'm afraid."

Alice felt herself deflate. She knew that school budgets were tight everywhere, but the room was barely fit for habitation.

"The whole building is falling apart." Lucy nodded at the school behind them. "All the money we do have is going to maintenance to keep things running. The heating only works half the time, and when it does it's at about twenty percent capacity. And the lights flicker all the time. It's not so bad on sunny days, but when it's dark it can be a real pain."

"I see." Alice suddenly longed for her ultra-modern, inner-city school in Manchester.

"Bet Hardaker never told you any of this when you came for the interview."

"Indeed, he didn't," Alice agreed. She glanced at the old building, realising she should have known it was falling apart when she first saw it.

"He's a little economical with the truth sometimes," Lucy confessed, "but on the bright side, he lets us do whatever we want. So, if you did want to decorate, he certainly wouldn't stop you, but he'd not be able to finance it."

Alice thought about her form room. It was in serious need of some maintenance and then some decorating. She had no idea how much time or money it would take, but she didn't relish the idea of spending her own funds on either.

"Colin Whittaker!" Lucy bellowed.

Alice jumped at the sudden sound. For a small woman, Lucy had an impressive set of lungs.

Colin instantly dropped the small branch he was holding as he chased some girls.

"You know Colin?" Alice asked.

"Yes, his older brother, Matthew, is in my class. If Colin is anything like his brother, and it seems he is, he'll be trouble." Lucy continued to glare at Colin, warning him with her eyes.

"He has tried to push my authority a couple of times," Alice confessed.

"Same as his brother then," Lucy said. "Matthew is a bully; that often runs in the family. Their parents are the landlords of the Flower Pot Pub up on the A Road into town."

Alice wasn't surprised that Lucy knew that. In fact, she imagined that Lucy knew everyone in town.

"Do you know Rose Hall?" Alice asked, her thoughts fading back to the shy youngster.

"Rosie, yes, that's Hannah's daughter," Lucy explained. "Hannah Hall was in my younger sister's class. She had a bit of a rough time in school, but she didn't make it any easier on herself. Nowadays, she's a single mum and works at one of the hairdressers in town. I don't know much about Rosie; Hannah kind of keeps to herself."

"She's been very quiet in class," Alice said, wondering if the lack of desire for social interaction was a family trait.

"Hannah's always been… interesting," Lucy said, her gaze still firmly fixed on the playground. "She never had any friends at school, a bit of a loner. Then there was this thing with her mum, now that was a day!"

Alice shifted uncomfortably as Lucy drifted into what she considered speculative gossip. Before Lucy had the chance to say any more, Alice caught sight of Colin tiptoeing towards a girl with a handful of soil in his cupped hands.

"Colin Whittaker!" Alice shouted.

"Colin, go to Mr Hardaker's office, now!" Lucy commanded.

Colin dropped the soil and trudged towards the school.

"We'll talk more about the locals later," Lucy promised with a grin and a wink.

Alice gave a half-hearted smile and nodded. She didn't want to talk about the locals. Her one concern with a small town was that everyone would know everyone else's business, which definitely seemed to be the case. Alice liked to make her own decisions about people and not prejudge them based upon stories she'd heard in whispers.

How to bring that up with Lucy without offending her would be difficult but, seeing as Lucy was the only person who had reached out to her yet, she might just have to.

She pushed her hands into her coat pockets and looked around the playground, checking for anything that needed her attention.

5

AN ENCYCLOPAEDIA HOUSED IN A LEMON CARDIGAN

HANNAH WAITED OUTSIDE THE GATES. The bell indicating the end of the day had rung a few minutes earlier, and there was a stream of children rushing out of the main doors.

In her own school days, she'd always been one of the first out, desperate to get home. She hoped Rosie wouldn't think that way. She wanted school to be a better experience for her daughter, which was why she had tried to instil a sense of fun and excitement in her when it came to learning. She didn't know if it was that or if Rosie was genetically predisposed to enjoy acquiring new knowledge. Either way, she hoped the school environment was everything Rosie had hoped it would be.

Just then, Rosie appeared in the doorway, her rucksack visible almost before she was. Hannah waved, and Rosie turtle-waddled over to her.

"Did you have a good day, pumpkin?" Hannah bent down and wrapped her arms around her daughter.

"It was great. We did all the school rules and we spoke

about reading and we got some new textbooks. We're allowed to decorate them." Rosie pulled back and looked intently at her mother. "I don't think I want to decorate mine."

"Maybe think about it?" Hannah suggested. "You might think of something that would be perfect."

She stood up and gently tugged the rucksack from Rosie's shoulders. She worried the girl would tip over with the added weight.

"Maybe. Miss Spencer says we get another textbook tomorrow."

"Another one?" Hannah enthused for Rosie's benefit. "Maybe we should get you a trolley instead of a bag?"

"That's silly," Rosie informed her.

"True." Hannah held out her hand, and Rosie took it.

"Miss Spencer said we are going to make up stories tomorrow."

"Did she?"

"Yes. We are going to work in groups. Miss Spencer says that there will be gold stars given out for the best stories."

"Wow, do you think you'll get a gold star?" Hannah smiled at the fact that Miss Spencer had been mentioned three times within a single minute. She gestured that they should start walking back towards the village, guessing that Rosie would happily stand outside the gate and talk about Miss Spencer and her first day of school for the next few hours if allowed.

Rosie shrugged her shoulders.

"Do you want some help thinking of a story?" Hannah asked.

"No, I have a story."

"Do you think it's not very good?" Hannah fished.

"No, I think it's good. I just don't want to say it out loud to everyone."

"Ah." Hannah figured as much.

She knew Rosie would struggle a little with the group activities, but she'd hoped that the excitement of her first day would have helped with that. It seemed that Rosie hadn't said a lot in class and didn't plan to.

"Are we going back to the salon now?" Rosie asked.

"Nope."

Rosie looked up at her curiously. She was used to Hannah's schedule, even if the hours sometimes changed, she was mostly working.

"I have the whole afternoon off," Hannah announced, unable to stop her grin. "And we are—"

"Mummy, don't tease!" Rosie bounced up and down in anticipation of the surprise.

"We are," Hannah said again for emphasis, "going to...

"Mummy!" Rosie whined.

"The library," Hannah finished.

Rosie's eyes opened wide, and a shout of joy erupted from her lips. She started to skip on the spot. Hannah had never been one for reading, but it had become quickly apparent that Rosie adored it. The only affordable way to keep up with her appetite for new books was to take frequent trips to the library. Unfortunately, they weren't always as frequent as Hannah, or Rosie, would have liked.

"And then," Hannah continued, "we're going to the supermarket to get ingredients for pizza!"

Hannah would have thought it was impossible for Rosie to get more excited, but she did just that as she let out a squeal. Pizza was Rosie's favourite meal, and she loved to help to make it.

A trip to the library and a homemade pizza weren't much by most people's standards, but it was all Hannah could manage. She was pleased that it made Rosie deliriously happy, so she guessed that it was enough.

They walked farther into town in silence, Hannah thinking about what she needed at the shop while Rosie skipped beside her.

"Daniel cried in class," Rosie suddenly announced.

"Why?"

"He thought school was just one day," Rosie explained. "When Miss Spencer said she'd see us all tomorrow, he didn't get why. So, she told him he'd be in school until he was sixteen. He cried."

Hannah smothered a laugh. She worried about that boy. She'd been pretty bad in school, but Daniel was the dumbest kid she'd ever known.

"What did Miss Spencer say to that?" Hannah asked.

"She said that he'd get used to it. She said he might enjoy it and want to stay even longer."

Hannah laughed. She couldn't see it somehow.

"Do you like Miss Spencer?" she asked.

"Yes. She's nice."

"Good. Not hairy?"

"No. And no big teeth," Rosie said.

"Bet she still has the eye in the back of her head," Hannah teased.

Hannah strolled around the library, trying to contain her boredom. The building was small, and she'd circled every set of shelves at least ten times. Every now and then she reached out and considered a book before remembering how little time she had. Not to mention the fact she didn't particularly enjoy reading. It had always been something she had been forced to do, and something she'd been bad at.

Thankfully, Rosie had never had that problem. Rosie was interested in books long before she could properly hold one, and Hannah had done her best to feed that interest. Which was why she was in a library with a five-year-old who had read almost all the books in the puny children's section.

Mrs Lawrence, the librarian, was on hand to help Rosie with new books she might want to try. She had even gone so far as to order in books from other libraries once or twice. It was a relief as Hannah really had no idea what Rosie should be reading or who wrote what. But Mrs Lawrence was an encyclopaedia housed in a lemon cardigan, and she loved Rosie.

Hannah walked past the reception desk where Mrs Lawrence was happily scanning Rosie's new stash of books.

"Miss Spencer said we're getting homework tomorrow," Rosie said. "I've never had homework."

"Homework? You're too young to have homework," Mrs Lawrence decided.

"I want homework," Rosie confessed. "I like it."

"It's true," Hannah said. "She's asked me to assign her homework in the past."

Mrs Lawrence shook her head. "Growing up too fast," she mumbled.

Hannah agreed. Rosie was growing up too fast. She wished she had some kind of magic potion that would allow her to slow things down and enjoy more time with her daughter while she was a child. It seemed like every time she turned around, Rosie had done a little more growing up.

"I hope it's maths," Rosie said.

Hannah chuckled. Only her daughter would be *wishing* for math homework.

6

THE MUCH-TALKED-ABOUT MISS SPENCER

As ALICE PACKED up her things, she felt relieved that the day had gone surprisingly well. A couple of minor meltdowns were always to be expected, and both had been easily dealt with. She walked around the room, tucking chairs under desks and straightening things up. She knew the cleaners would be in soon, but she wanted to leave the room as presentable as possible.

She shivered as she passed the window, the wooden surround having rotted so much that air was blowing through.

"This is ridiculous," she muttered to herself.

She grabbed her bag and decided to go and see the headmaster. Lucy had said there was no money in the budget for decorating, but some of the repairs were beyond superficial. At least if she brought it up with Hardaker herself, she'd know she'd done all she could.

She exited the classroom and headed towards the stairs, her footsteps echoing down the long corridor. She looked into the other rooms as she passed. All looked similar, but none were quite as bland and run-down as hers. She assumed other teachers had held onto their previous forms' work in order to decorate the bare walls.

As she walked down the stairs and towards the headmaster's office, she thought about what she wanted to say. She had to be clear and concise. This wasn't simply about aesthetics, although that was important. She had to highlight the state of decay and the fact that it was uncomfortable and possibly even dangerous to the students.

Hardaker was leaving his office when she arrived. In her old school, most teachers didn't go home until at least two hours after the end of the children's school day. Often the headmaster stayed even longer.

Things were very different in Fairlight.

"Headmaster, if I may have a word?"

Hardaker looked at her and then at his watch. "It will have to be a quick one, Miss Spencer. I promised my wife I would be home at a reasonable hour, and I'm already late."

Alice blinked. The only way he could have left any earlier was if he left with the children. *Twenty* minutes ago.

"I do hope you've not had enough of us already?" he asked with a jovial chuckle.

"Oh, no, nothing like that. But I do need to talk to you about my form room. It's in dire need of maintenance."

Hardaker stepped around her and started walking. She fell into step behind him. He was old, but he was fast when he wanted to get home.

"As is the entire school, my dear," he said.

"There are draughts, and the lights dimmed for around an hour this afternoon," Alice explained.

"We have an electrician coming soon."

"And the draughts?"

"It's an old building." Hardaker shrugged. "It can't be helped."

"With respect, headmaster, I think it's detrimental to the children's learning and possibly to their health."

"A nice winter coat and they will be fine," Hardaker reassured her. He paused and turned to face her. "Most of the village and surrounding villages attended this school. You don't see uneducated masses lying in the streets, suffering with consumption."

Alice stood her ground. "Well, no, but we don't know how much stronger their education might have been if they'd been taught in a building that had been better maintained."

"My dear, I'd like nothing more than to fix the whole building, but there simply isn't any money. If a window falls out, of course it will be replaced. If there is a danger to the children, it will be repaired. But draughts and holes in brickwork are simply not a priority. Is there anything else?"

Alice knew there was no point in trying to reason with him. He hadn't seen the effects of a modern, inspiring working environment like she had. She didn't want to cause too much trouble on her first day. She might need Hardaker on her side for other things in the future. This wasn't a battle she would win today.

"No, headmaster, thank you for your time."

He nodded, seemingly happy that the matter had been resolved. He turned and headed towards the door.

"Of course," he called over his shoulder, "you are welcome to decorate in whatever way you see fit. At your own expense, naturally. If you feel it would help the children."

Alice ground her teeth. "Thank you, headmaster," she called back.

She shook her head. Of course, she knew budgets were tight, but it was obvious that Hardaker was completely disinterested in trying to make real improvements. He was focused on making the building just about habitable, not a place where children would thrive.

No child was going to feel good about coming to a freezing, bland box of a classroom, and no person, adult or child, would be able to focus on learning in such conditions. She reminded herself that it was September and that it would only get worse. The very thought of January in the form room was enough to make her shiver.

Clattering behind her caused her to turn around. A cleaner was manhandling an old vacuum cleaner into the hallway. She looked at Alice in surprise.

"You're here late, miss," she said.

Alice had never finished a school day so early, but it seemed a frequent occurrence in Fairlight to get out of the door shortly after the children.

"Just leaving now," she said. "Have a nice night."

She exited the building and headed towards the car park. On the way, she wondered if she could get the children to create some art for the walls without it getting in the way of their curriculum. She also wondered how effective flimsy paper would be against actual holes in the wall.

Hardaker was in the car park, a grin on his face.

"I had one of these, many years ago." He pointed to her car.

"It's a classic," she replied as she unlocked her racing green original Mini.

"Many, many years ago," he continued. "Not sure when, was it the early seventies?"

Alice assumed she wasn't part of the conversation anymore and put her bag on the passenger seat. She noticed the car park was completely empty aside from a Volvo, which she assumed belonged to Hardaker. It seemed they were the last two out of the building.

"This one is from the late eighties," she replied.

"Well, I hope it doesn't cause you too many problems," he said.

"None so far," she said.

Probably because I maintain it better than you maintain your school, she thought.

"Good, good. Well, I better go. See you in the morning," he said.

"Absolutely, have a nice evening." She got into the car and closed the door, letting out a deep breath.

She had known that starting a new job would be stressful and that there would be lots of things to learn, especially in such a small town. It was obvious that things would be different. She was just a little taken aback by how different they were.

"When in Rome," she mumbled and started the engine.

Alice parked up at the local supermarket. It was about a fiftieth of the size she was used to, but she assumed, and hoped, she would be able to find everything she needed. According to Google Maps, Fairlight had a corner shop and a supermarket. The next nearest supermarket was a twenty-minute drive away, not terrible but not convenient for a pint of milk.

She got out of the car, noticing that a few passers-by were gawking at her. She was used to her classic car attracting attention, but she had to wonder in this instance if it was the car or her. Fairlight seemed pretty small, and she got the impression that anyone new was going to warrant a second look.

Basket in hand, she strolled around the supermarket aisles. It was a pleasant surprise that that the supermarket has a TARDIS feel to it, seemingly containing more inside than looked possible from the outside.

She turned a corner and saw a woman and a small girl whom she recognised as Rosie Hall. Rosie saw her and subtly positioned herself behind the woman's legs in an attempt to hide. Alice tilted her head to the side to catch Rosie's line of vision and smiled.

It was then that the woman noticed her and looked at her strangely.

Alice realised that she was staring, and *smiling,* at a stranger's legs.

I'm sorry, I'm not looking at your legs," Alice apologised. She closed her eyes for a second as she realised how ridiculous that sounded. "I mean, I am... but."

She stopped talking and took a breath to gather her thoughts. She looked up and made eye contact with the woman. Her breath caught in her throat for a moment. The woman was gorgeous with long, flowing, brown hair and rich brown eyes. She wore tight jeans and a cosy knitted sweater that complimented her figure. She shook her head, trying to piece her thoughts together.

"I'm Rosie's teacher," she finally explained.

"Ah, the much-talked-about Miss Spencer. I'm Hannah, Rosie's mum."

Hannah held out her hand, and Alice shook it. She was glad to hear that Rosie had spoken about her, and the smile on Hannah's face suggested that what she had said was positive.

Hannah stepped to the side a little, forcing Rosie to make eye contact with her teacher. Alice looked at Rosie and then at Hannah, realising that Rosie was quite simply a tiny version of her mother. Of course, it was common for children to look like their parents, but the similarities were startling.

"We're just buying the ingredients for pizza," Hannah explained when the silence dragged on a little.

"That sounds lovely. Pizza is one of my favourites," Alice said, addressing Rosie in the hope that she'd coax her out of her shell.

Rosie smiled but silently hugged her mother's leg.

"It's Rosie's absolute favourite. It's a celebration for the first day of school."

"What a good idea! Did you have a good day, Rosie?" Alice asked.

Rosie nodded her head eagerly but still remained voiceless.

"Wonderful, me too. But I better let you get on," Alice said, knowing that Rosie was a little uncomfortable. She looked at Hannah, the air briefly leaving her lungs as the young woman made eye contact with her and smiled.

"It was lovely meeting you," Alice said.

"And you."

Alice nodded and walked into another aisle. She didn't need any baby food or formula, which seemed to be its primary contents, but she needed to get away from Hannah. The woman was effortlessly stunning, and her smile lifted Alice up to new heights. She wanted more of that smile, even though she knew it wasn't possible. Rosie's presence indicated that Alice was barking up the wrong tree.

Not to mention that it had been so long since Alice had been in a relationship that she had completely forgotten what to do. The idea of asking someone out was terrifying, especially on her first working day in a new town, with a presumably straight woman who was the parent of one of her students. Not to mention much younger than her.

But Hannah's smile had entranced her in a few short seconds. Alice didn't know what it was about her. Yes, she was attractive, but there was something else. It felt like a bolt of lightning had struck Alice's heart.

You've been single too long, Alice told herself.

She looked up and saw Rosie and Hannah walking towards another aisle. Alice closed her eyes for a second before she shook her head and turned away. Her heart's ability to become infatuated by the absolutely least likely person to be interested in her continued to amaze her.

She walked to the food aisle and started gathering ingredients for dinner, casually wondering if she should just grab a ready meal for one. The thought was appealing in that it saved time and effort, but it was awful for her self-esteem.

She reminded herself that it was her first week in Fairlight. Things would get better. Hopefully, she'd soon make some friends, and in the future, who knew?

7

THE FAIRLIGHT GRAPEVINE

ROSIE SAT ON THE SOFA, a pile of books on the coffee table in front of her, her chosen book in her hands. Hannah sat at the dining table with all her home admin paperwork strewn over the table top. She glanced up at her daughter.

"You can watch a DVD if you like," she offered.

"No, I'm happy reading," Rosie replied.

Hannah chuckled and shook her head. At Rosie's age, television time had been Hannah's most coveted pastime. Anything to be sucked out of reality and rest her brain for a while. She supposed Rosie was technically doing the same, just in a different way.

To give her eyes a break from the various forms, she looked out the window. Below, people were wrapped up in winter coats and hurrying along the street. It had become unseasonably cold very suddenly. Apparently, summer had abandoned England early this year.

The thought of long winter nights made Hannah worry about just how much time Rosie spent indoors.

Given the choice, her daughter always preferred to stay in the apartment with a book. This was good for her education, but not great for her health.

Hannah picked up her phone and searched for things to do with children during the winter time. A few suggestions popped up, and swimming caught her eye. It had been years since she'd gone swimming.

A check of the local council website revealed that the local pool was a thirty-minute bus journey away and that the cost wasn't too expensive. She mentally calculated how many extra appointments she would need to book in order to cover the cost of a weekly swimming session for them both.

"Rosie? How do you feel about going swimming? If Mummy can get the money together?"

Rosie lowered her book and turned her head. "Really?"

"Really," Hannah agreed, seeing that Rosie was interested in the idea.

"That sounds like fun," Rosie agreed.

"I'll see what I can do," Hannah said.

She knew not to make promises she couldn't keep, and Rosie knew not to expect too much. For a child, she had a good understanding that things cost money and money wasn't always plentiful.

Hannah wished it wasn't that way. She wished that Rosie could have everything she wanted, but reality was a fun-sapping mistress.

She picked up her phone and sent off a quick text to Adrian requesting any extra shifts. He was a fantastic salesman and could often manage to get the locals to come in slightly earlier than they might have done. The previous

November he had managed to rustle up five new appointments just by casually commenting to someone in the post office that they were already booked solid for Christmas haircuts.

Of course, everyone decided that they needed another haircut before Christmas, and Adrian was more than happy to squeeze them into a supposedly packed schedule.

As she sent the text to Adrian, she received an email notification from her father. She thumbed open the message. It was the same thing he sent every month, claiming that the money paid directly into her account was pocket money for Rosie. He signed off saying he wanted more photographs of his two favourite girls.

Hannah laughed to herself. She sent about three photos a day to her father, but he always claimed that he never received enough.

She replied, thanking him for the money and telling him he really shouldn't have. She added, in response to his request for more photos, that he could always come and visit. She knew Fairlight was a long way from Scotland and that they didn't have the room to put him up, but the offer was always open to him.

Some nights she wondered if she should have gone with him to Scotland, what their lives would have been like up north. But she'd chosen to stay in Fairlight, where she had a job and a couple of good friends. She might have hated Fairlight, but it was her home and she couldn't imagine being anywhere else.

"Mummy?" Rosie asked from the living room.

"Yes, pumpkin?"

"What kind of homework do you think I'll have?"

Ah. Her mind was still on school. Hannah lowered her phone and made a big show of thinking about the question.

"Building a rocket," she decided. "A real one. So that you and Miss Spencer can go to the moon."

Rosie laughed. "That sounds very silly. I hope it's more reading."

"I don't think you have time for any more reading," Hannah told her. "You'll go blind."

"If my bedtime was later, then I'd have more time for reading," Rosie tried.

"Ah, I see. It's the bedtime discussion again. Nice try, but bedtime is seven-thirty and no later. If your home-work is reading, then you'll have to read your homework first and then your other books in whatever time is left."

Rosie sighed and turned back to her book, obviously disappointed at failing in her goal to extend her reading time.

"You'll thank me one day," Hannah told her.

Rosie remained quiet.

"Even if it's not today," Hannah mumbled to herself.

She'd have given anything for a fixed bedtime when she was growing up. Her father was often away for work for many weeks at a time, and her mother didn't even know she was there. She never went to bed, often passing out from exhaustion on her bedroom floor at some point during the evening or the early morning.

"It's not fair," Rosie muttered into the pages of her book.

Hannah walked over to her. She stood behind the sofa

and placed her hand on her daughter's head, gently running her fingers through her hair.

"One day, you'll understand. I might be accused of coddling you, but never of not loving or caring for you."

Rosie paused in her reading and turned around to look up at her. She didn't understand. Hannah had never told her much about her own childhood. Rosie never asked, too young to be curious.

But Rosie obviously knew that something was up. "I love you," she said.

"I love you, too." Hannah looked up at the clock on the wall. "Five minutes until bedtime."

Rosie let out a heartfelt groan.

Hannah placed the last item of clothing on the pile. She hated ironing. She didn't think there were many people who enjoyed it, but she hated it with a passion. The irritating task was about to double with Rosie's uniform being added to the mix.

She looked at her watch. It was ten o'clock, and she'd just managed to finish all the chores.

Not that she minded. She'd stay up until any time to ensure Rosie had a freshly ironed school outfit and a packed lunch ready to go in the morning. She shook her head at the sham that had been this particular morning. She couldn't believe that Rosie had prepared her own lunch. Just because she was exceptionally able didn't mean she should be doing so.

Now, no matter what hurry she was in the following

morning, she'd know that Rosie would find a lunch ready for her in the fridge.

Her phone vibrated in her pocket. She saw it was her father and quickly answered the call.

"Hello, darling," he greeted. "I wanted to ask how Rosie's first day at school went."

"It was great, she loved it."

"Good, good. There was no doubt about that, bright girl like her. No problems, then?"

Hannah knew what he was alluding to. She felt sorry for him. He'd had no idea of the terrible conditions Hannah had endured until everything had come to a head. Years had gone by with him only half aware of what was happening at home. Even with that fifty-percent knowledge, he never acted. She knew he felt guilty about that now, but she didn't want him to. Blame could be spread around quite widely, but Hannah knew it wouldn't change the past.

"No problems," she said breezily. "She was a bit quiet, but that's Rosie. She liked her teacher."

"That's good. And how about you?"

"I… missed her. But I know I'll get used to it," she admitted. "And it will mean less time she has to hang out in the salon."

"That will be much better for both of you. I'll give her a call later this week, but I wanted to ask you first."

He loved to chat on the phone, but Rosie wasn't so keen. It had taken him a while to understand that difference between them. Nowadays, he called Hannah first to get the information he wanted and then had a casual chat with Rosie after.

"I appreciate that. I'm sure she won't say a lot, you know what she's like," Hannah said.

"She's like you were when you were little. Didn't have a lot to say."

"That's all changed now, though, right?" she joked.

"Yep, now I can't stop you."

She smiled, enjoying their banter.

"Guess what Rosie did this morning?" she said.

"What did she do?"

"She made her own lunch."

He laughed. "I'm surprised she didn't take herself to school. She's been looking forward to it since she could say the word."

"I know! I was a little behind this morning—"

"—as usual."

"As usual," she confessed. "And when I saw her, she was fully dressed, with her bag packed and a lunch made and put in her lunchbox."

"That's my granddaughter. She'll go far."

"She will. I just hope she doesn't leave me behind. She's five. She shouldn't be making her own lunch at five."

"She can come and make my dinner if she likes?" he joked.

"We have a rule about using the oven or the microwave only when I'm in the room," she explained.

"Good. She has a wise head on young shoulders, but she's still a wee thing. Has she grown at all yet?"

"No, still waiting on that growth spurt so she can see her fingers through her school jumper." Hannah unplugged the iron and started putting things away in the kitchen. "I've made her lunch now and put it in the fridge, so she doesn't make her own again."

"Keeps you on your toes, doesn't she?"

"She really does!"

"You say she likes her teacher?"

"Yes, Miss Spencer was mentioned a lot throughout the afternoon and evening."

Hannah's mind started to wander. She'd tried to forget about the gorgeous woman in the supermarket, but it wasn't easy when Rosie mentioned her in every other breath.

"Spencer? Don't remember that name."

"She's new to the area. I think someone said she's from Manchester?"

"Ah! The Fairlight Grapevine. They'll know her inside leg measurement within a day or two." He chuckled.

Hannah bit her lip. "Yeah," she said half-heartedly.

She didn't want to think about Miss Spencer's inner leg. Or any part of her legs for that matter. There was probably a Mr Spencer who would disapprove of that. Not to mention that she shouldn't be objectifying Rosie's teacher.

Her mind unhelpfully replayed the scene in the supermarket. *I'm sorry, I'm not looking at your legs.* Hannah smiled at the clumsy comment. The blush that had risen on the teacher's cheeks had been adorable. It had taken all her self-control to not giggle at it.

"It's weird how we call teachers 'mister' and 'miss'," she said.

"Goes back to the old days, a mark of respect," he said.

"True, but we still do it and many other countries

don't. I remember thinking of my teachers as not quite real people. Like they had a stage name and I knew nothing about their real life," Hannah said. "Like, I remember all the girls in my class wondering if Mr Dingwall was married or not. Or what his first name was."

"Yes, I remember when you found out his name was Hector. I think you and your friends laughed for about a week."

"Hector Dingwall," Hannah chuckled. "Whatever happened to him?"

"Died in a crash on the A218."

Hannah's shoulders slumped. "Thanks, Dad. Way to kill a conversation."

"Not my fault. He *did* die in a crash on the A218."

She laughed and shook her head. "I better go; it's late and it's a school night."

"Of course, I just wanted to see how everything went."

"You need to come down and see us soon, okay?" she told him.

"I know, I'm working out some dates."

"Good, I miss you, Daddy."

"I miss you, too."

She hung up the call and put the phone back in her pocket. The conversation hadn't helped her get rid her thoughts of Miss Spencer. She supposed she'd never be able to, at least not for the next school year.

She'd just have to hope that Rosie never got into any trouble that warranted her being called into the school. A smile curled at her lips at the very thought of Rosie ever getting in trouble.

Her best bet was to push thoughts of Miss Spencer

aside. Yes, she was attractive, but it had to stop there. She was probably married, and even if she wasn't, she was most likely straight.

Not to mention the fact that Hannah was in no way ready for a relationship. She could barely keep her life together, never mind think about dating anyone. She had put the whole idea on the back burner until Rosie was much older.

A small voice, which sounded suspiciously like her father's, told her that she was being a coward. Pushing the idea of finding a partner to one side until Rosie was older was something he strongly disagreed with, but then she supposed that every parent wanted to see their adult children in a happy relationship and to have someone to lean on.

Hannah would like that, too, but she knew that the road to a relationship ran a high risk of rejection. Especially when you were a single mother with a chip on your shoulder and the entire town around you had stories from your childhood to tell whomever asked.

It was easier to remain alone.

8

NO ROOM FOR A DADDY

ALICE MENTALLY COUNTED children as she greeted them on their way back in from lunch. They were noisy and excitable, most of them starting to come out of their shells and push the boundaries a little more.

They took their seats, and she stood silently at the front of the classroom, waiting for them to notice her and quieten down. Despite there only being twelve of them, it took a while for them to realise that she was waiting for them and to sit nicely and stop talking.

"When you come back to class," she said, "I expect you to do so quickly and quietly. Does everyone understand?"

"Yes, Miss Spencer."

"Good. Now, for this lesson, I need everyone to stand up and follow me."

She enjoyed the puzzled expressions on their faces as they all stood up and looked to each other in confusion. She led her students along the corridor and down the stairs, occasionally turning to remind them to stay quiet as other classes were in session.

Downstairs, she led them to a large wooden door.

"There's a library?" Simone asked, reading the gold-leafed lettering on the door.

"There is," Alice confirmed. She opened the door, switched on the lights, and gestured for the children to go inside.

She'd had a brief look at the room while the children were on their lunch break. It was a reasonable size, although for some inexplicable reason it was in the middle of the building, with no windows to provide natural light.

The shelves were extremely old and made of sturdy, dark mahogany. While most of the books were outdated, the library was fairly well stocked.

She scrunched up her nose. Also, there was a strange smell, yet another interesting peculiarity the school had.

The children were looking around the room with interest. She noticed that Rosie Hall seemed particularly happy as she ran her fingers along the spines.

"Feel free to have a look around," Alice instructed.

Sometimes it was a good idea to give the children some freedom and to walk amongst them to see what could be overheard. She wondered if it was a good time to approach Rosie. While Alice understood that she was shy, the young girl was now the only student who hadn't spoken directly to her.

It was a delicate situation. Sometimes a shy student appreciated an approach from their teacher. Sometimes it was the wrong thing entirely and pushed the child into clamming up even more.

Alice stood near to Rosie, close enough that she could talk if she desired but also in a position that looked like she was simply watching over the class.

Rosie was looking through books on a low shelf when a boy called Quentin approached her. Alice had noticed that Quentin was a rather boastful boy who hadn't learnt some of the finer aspects of socialising yet.

"My daddy has built me even more bookshelves because I have *sooo* many books," he told Rosie.

Alice tried to maintain a neutral expression and not roll her eyes despite Quentin's obvious brag.

"I don't have a daddy," Rosie replied evenly.

"I have two," he said. "A black one and a white one. You can borrow one if you like?"

Alice smothered her snort of laughter behind her hand and tried to look like she wasn't eavesdropping.

"That's nice of you, but I don't think I want a daddy. And we don't really have room to keep one."

Alice took a step away, so she was behind the bookshelf so that neither child could catch her chuckling.

"They are pretty good," Quentin admitted. "If you need bookshelves."

"I don't need any bookshelves. I get all my books from the library. I always have room for more books."

"But no daddy?" Quentin asked.

"No, just me and Mummy."

That was confirmation on Lucy's earlier comment about Hannah being a single mum. She couldn't help but wonder what the story was there. Obviously, there were many single parents all around the world, but curiosity often made her wonder what circumstances had led up to the arrangement. Not that it mattered. She found herself quite pleased to learn that there was no Mr Hall in the picture.

Looking up, she noticed that Colin was speaking to Simone and that the girl was starting to look upset. Alice pushed herself away from the shelves and walked over to them. As soon as Colin saw her arrive, he went suspiciously quiet.

"Everything okay here?" Alice asked.

"Yes, miss," Colin said quickly.

Alice fixed Simone with a friendly look. "Simone?"

Simone nodded her head, obviously not wanting to elaborate on whatever it was she had missed.

Alice gave Colin one last look, letting him know that she was watching him. Even without Lucy's comments, she would have known that Colin was trouble waiting to happen. She turned around.

"Class, class," she said, waiting for them to settle and look towards her. "I want each of you to pick one book that you will sign out of the library. You'll read the book during silent reading time in the classroom, and you'll also take it home and will read it for homework."

She paused to allow the groans to subside. Luckily, they came from just a couple of the boys who were already complaining about the idea of homework.

"Thank you for your enthusiasm," she said playfully. "Now, choose a book and see me at the front desk. I'll show you how we sign books out."

She took a seat at the desk and opened up the old library log, immediately missing the electronic system at her old school. Willows School wasn't simply underfunded. It was stuck in the dark ages with no desire to progress.

A large book landed on the desk. She looked up at Daniel, and then at the book.

"What did you choose, Daniel?" she asked.

"A book."

"Which book is it?" she tried again. She already knew she'd earn her salary with Daniel this year.

"I dunno." He shrugged his shoulders.

She picked up the world atlas and put it to one side. "Might I suggest that you go to the section over there and have a look at those books? Look at the cover and read the back to see what the book is about. You might find something a little more suitable there."

"Okay." He turned and walked away.

As time went on, she learnt more and more about the children. Colin was a potential troublemaker. Simone was loud at times. Daniel was either challenged or unaware of the world around him. Rosie was shy. Quentin was a horrible brag.

It was fascinating to see their personalities starting to shine through and to decide what she needed to do in order to help them excel. No two children were the same, she passionately believed that each child needed a personal touch in order to thrive.

She was pulled out of her reflection by a cry and a thud. Colin was standing over Simone, having obviously just pushed her.

"Colin! Go to the headmaster's office right now," Alice instructed as she jumped to her feet. By the time she got to Simone, the girl was already standing back up.

Alice crouched down and quickly checked her over for injuries. "Are you hurt?"

"No, miss."

"What happened?"

Simone made a face. "Colin is just mean."

Alice turned around to see the boy strolling towards the door as if he had all the time in the world.

"Colin, do not test me," she warned.

He picked up the pace and disappeared into the corridor.

She looked at Simone. "Are you sure you're okay?"

"Yes."

"If he does anything like that again or says anything you don't like, you come to me or one of the other teachers, okay?"

Simone gave a half-hearted nod.

Alice stood up and addressed the rest of the class. "As per the rules we agreed on yesterday, we treat each other with respect. We do not say mean things, and we most certainly never push each other. It won't be tolerated. Do you all understand?"

The children nodded.

"Right, good. Let's put this behind us and choose some nice books to read."

She sat back down, wondering what had caused Colin's behaviour or if it was normal acting out for attention and control. Whatever it was, she needed to figure it out and put a stop to it.

9

HOMEWORK AT LAST

HANNAH WAITED ANXIOUSLY by the school gate. She had to hurry back to the salon to deal with grumpy Mrs Harper. Like many of her clients in Fairlight, Mrs Harper was retired and had all the time in the world. However, she always wanted her appointment at the most inconvenient time. She also hated to be kept waiting and had a terrible habit of arriving early to her appointment.

Adrian was with another client or else he would have picked Rosie up to allow Hannah to wait for Mrs Harper's arrival.

Hannah knew that it didn't matter if she hurried or if she dawdled. When she got back to the salon, Mrs Harper would be waiting. She was convinced the old battleaxe hid around the corner and waited for Hannah to step out of the salon, just to get in her status quo of complaints for the day.

Still, she wanted to minimise the amount of friction and hurry back.

Despite her time concerns, she couldn't help the smile

that overtook her face when Rosie appeared, still weighed down by a ridiculously overpacked rucksack. She'd need to have a talk with her about that. None of the other children seemed to have a bag twice their size strapped to their backs.

"Mummy, I have homework!" Rosie announced gleefully as she threw herself against Hannah's legs.

"Wow, that's great news." Hannah bent down and did up Rosie's coat. "Come on, pumpkin, we have to get going."

"It's reading! The school has a library. Did you know the school had a library?"

Hannah couldn't remember a library, but then again, she had spent years trying to rid herself of all memories of that time in her life.

"I'm not sure." She took Rosie's hand, and they walked up the street.

Hannah found herself glancing over her shoulder, wondering if she'd catch a peek of Miss Spencer. She made eye contact with one of the other teachers, Lucy Gibson, and quickly looked away.

"I have to write in my homework journal what I read," Rosie continued. "Miss Spencer wants us to read the book we got from the library for fifteen minutes and then write down anything else we read."

"I hope it's a big journal," Hannah quipped.

"Why are we hurrying?" Rosie asked.

"I have an appointment with Mrs Harper."

"Oh."

"Yes, oh. She's probably already there and looking very grumpy."

"Why is she always grumpy?" Rosie asked.

"I think she enjoys it."

"How can anyone enjoy being grumpy?"

"Some people do. Some people prefer to be grumpy rather than happy."

"That's silly," Rosie said.

"It is, but we're not those people. We just cut their hair. Well, I do. You'll be reading and having an afternoon snack. Unless you want to switch? If I got you a chair, you could stand on that and cut Mrs Harper's hair. What do you think?"

Rosie giggled. "No, I don't think so, Mummy."

"Oh, shame. Anyway, tell me how school was."

Rosie shrugged. "It was good."

"Did you tell your story?"

"No."

"No?" Hannah asked.

"No. I didn't want to."

Hannah could see the scene play out in her mind. Rosie probably had a story in mind but lost the courage to tell it to the class.

"Maybe another day," Hannah said, not wanting to push her too hard just yet. "How is Miss Spencer?"

"She's nice."

"Have you spoken to her yet?"

"No."

Hannah tried to remind herself that it was only the second day. There was still plenty of time for Rosie to gather her courage and actually start talking to her teacher and classmates.

They arrived at Chopz, and, sure enough, Mrs Harper

was waiting in reception looking miserable about it, despite the fact that she was fifteen minutes early for her appointment.

Hannah sent Rosie through to the staff room where she'd prepared a snack of vegetable sticks and dips for her. Rosie had spent so much time in the room that it was her home away from home.

Mrs Harper looked pointedly at her watch. Hannah knew better than to argue with her strange sense of time-keeping. Pointing out that she was early would just sour her mood further. The old woman had already threatened to go to the other hairdresser in town on a couple of occasions. As much as Hannah disliked her, she was a paying client, and that was more important.

This was especially true, seeing as Hannah's pool of clients was relatively small. She mainly dealt with the older people in town, the ones she hadn't attended school with. Now and then she styled hair for people her age and a little older, but as she did, all she could think about was what *they* were thinking about *her*. It was better for everyone if she stuck to the forty-and-over crowd. They were probably as judgemental and gossipy as the rest of them, but at least they had better acting skills than most.

As so often happened at Chopz, time rushed by.

Two back-to-back appointments were over before she knew it. Although she knew it would be a quick dinner and then practically straight to bed for Rosie, Hannah let out a sigh of relief that it was finally time to go home. The balance between earning money and having time with her daughter was still one she was working on.

She had grabbed the broom out of the closet and

started to sweep up the hair from her last appointment when Adrian grabbed the broom out of her hand.

"I'll do this, you head home."

Hannah shook her head and reached for the broom. "No, it's my client, my mess."

"My salon, my choice," Adrian pointed out. "You make me lunch tomorrow and we'll call it even."

She paused. She hated feeling like she wasn't pulling her weight, but getting home a few minutes earlier meant more time with Rosie.

"Are you sure?"

"Of course, get out of here."

Hannah didn't need to be told twice. She kissed his cheek. "You're a star, thank you."

She grabbed her coat and bag and popped her head around into the staff room. Rosie was reading, as usual.

"Pumpkin, time to go home."

Rosie nodded and placed her homemade bookmark into her book. "What's for dinner?"

"Whatever takes three and a half minutes to cook," Hannah replied, glancing at her watch.

"Sounds yummy," Rosie deadpanned.

Hannah helped her to pack up her. They hurried out of the salon and towards home.

"Quentin says I can have one of his daddies," Rosie said during the walk.

Hannah laughed. "I don't think he should be offering. You don't offer me to people, do you?"

"No. But you don't put up bookshelves."

"Oh, is that why he offered? Because his daddies put up bookshelves?"

"Yes. I told him I don't need any."

"Shelves or daddies?"

"Either."

"Damn right," Hannah mumbled through a grin.

Quentin was the adopted son of Lucas and Tom, the other gays in the village. Or rather, the other openly out gays. She had question marks over some people and wouldn't be at all surprised if they were choosing to live in the closet. Fairlight was a nosey town and everyone knew everyone else's business. Although, giving credit where it was due, she'd never experienced negative comments about being gay. Everything else, sure, but she'd never been the victim of any homophobic abuse. She imagined that there were some homophobes somewhere in the village, but thankfully, they kept to themselves.

Still, as safe as she felt being out, she knew she was a topic of conversation, and so were Lucas, Tom, and Quentin. Fairlight residents liked to talk about people, especially anyone who stood out.

Hannah sighed, shook her head, and unlocked the door.

"You need to sign my homework book," Rosie said as they took their coats off in the apartment hallway.

"Okay, I'll do it after dinner."

"You're supposed to test me to see if I read what I've said I read."

"That would mean that I'd have to read it, too," Hannah said, rummaging through the fridge for a healthy dinner that wouldn't take too long to prepare.

"Yes."

"We both know that isn't going to happen. So, you'll

just have to be honest with what you put in the homework book, or I'll tell Miss Spencer you lied, and she'll eat you."

Rosie laughed. "She won't. Miss Spencer is nice."

Hannah started preparing a chicken and potato salad. "She's nice now. But what if you lie on your homework book?"

"She will still be nice," Rosie decided with certainty.

Hannah was glad that Rosie had taken to Miss Spencer, even if she hadn't spoken to her directly yet. It was more than she had had when she was starting school.

The evening ran away from her, and Rosie was in bed much later than usual. Hannah knew that this would probably be the new normal now that Rosie was in school. She wondered if she could cut back on her late afternoon appointments or try to make a hot meal for Rosie while at the salon. There had to be a solution. Everything about their lives so far had been an uphill struggle and a hunt for solutions.

It was tough, but she knew she'd find one that worked for both of them.

She cleaned up the kitchen and wiped down its surfaces. On the edge of the counter was Rosie's homework book. She opened the page and saw that Rosie had finished the entire book she had picked up from the school library and started another book that she had picked up from the public library the day before. She chuckled to herself. *So much for fifteen minutes of reading.*

She signed the indicated box to agree that Rosie had read what she said she had and popped the book into Rosie's rucksack.

ROSIE OPENS UP

HANNAH HURRIED down the hill towards the school. A check of her watch told her that school had been out for just over five minutes. She was a little late after Mrs Perkins wanted to keep on talking about her twelve-year-old demon dog, Princess.

She weaved through the crowd of parents returning from the school gates with their kids, catching a few eye rolls as she did. She imagined most of the parents thought she was the worst mother in the world to be racing towards the gates after the bell had rung. Some were probably considering an anonymous tip to child services.

Upon entering the playground, she couldn't see Rosie anywhere. She looked around, in case Rosie had suddenly become interested in the climbing frame or talking to her classmates.

Nothing.

Panic was beginning to seep in when she saw Miss Spencer crossing the playground towards her.

"Miss Hall, I was wondering if you had a few moments to speak?" Miss Spencer asked.

"Rosie?" Hannah asked.

"She's still in the form room," Miss Spencer replied. "There's nothing wrong, I just wanted to have a quick chat."

Hannah couldn't remember a moment when a quick chat with a school teacher had been a good thing. She also couldn't remember a time she had ever managed to get out of one.

"Okay, sure," she said.

Miss Spencer smiled, and Hannah felt herself melt a little. She didn't know how someone could have such a warm smile. It even shone from her eyes.

She gestured for Hannah to follow her, and Hannah stepped into her old school for the first time in years. Dread crept up her spine. Miss Spencer was making small talk, apologising for the flicking lights in the stairwell, but Hannah was too busy facing down her demons to take in what was being said or to reply.

Her feet were heavy as they walked along the top corridor. She didn't know which room Rosie's form room was, but she had a strong suspicion that fate would play a cruel joke on her. Sure enough, Miss Spencer turned and led them into her old form room. The epicentre of all her school bullying.

"This room hasn't changed a bit," Hannah noted.

"Did you attend this school?" Miss Spencer asked.

"Unfortunately." Hannah looked around the room. It was just as run-down and miserable as she remembered.

The only bright spot was Rosie was sitting at a desk and reading her book. "Hey, pumpkin."

Rosie looked up and smiled.

Smiling, good, Hannah thought. *Can't be anything too bad.*

"Rosie, I'm going to have a chat with your mum. Carry on reading, we won't be long," Miss Spencer told her, taking a seat at her desk.

Hannah sat on the other side of the desk, where a chair had been provided. More flashbacks of school hit her.

"I'm sorry to drag you in," Miss Spencer said. "I just wanted to clarify some things in Rosie's homework book."

"Sure, okay." Hannah was happy to clarify anything if she could get out of the classroom as quickly as possible. Seeing more of Miss Spencer was pleasant. Doing so in the epicentre of her student nightmares was less so.

Miss Spencer opened Rosie's homework book which had been laying on her desk and turned it around for Hannah to see. Hannah took the book and looked at it. Everything looked the same as she had left it the night before.

"What's the problem?"

"Well, the homework I set was for fifteen minutes of reading, but Rosie has logged that she finished the book. She's also logged that she started another book."

"That's right." Hannah closed the homework book and handed it back. "She obviously read for more than fifteen minutes, as she put down in the book."

"I did notice that the time was written in by Rosie, which is a surprise as most of the children are soon to learn how to read a clock and tell the time. Did she fill that in under your instruction?"

Before Hannah had a chance to answer, Miss Spencer continued, "Also, both of these books are rather advanced for Rosie's age."

"She got the other book from the library in town. The librarian helped her pick it," Hannah explained. She felt a little defensive. Was Miss Spencer suggesting that Rosie wasn't reading age-appropriate books?

"If she is reading books at that level, then it's… well, it's extraordinary."

"She is. Reading books at that level. And extraordinary. She's always been bright," Hannah explained. "She loves to read. More than anything else."

Miss Spencer looked across the room to where Rosie sat. "I'm finding it hard to get her to speak to me," she said softly enough that Rosie wouldn't be able to hear. "I can't ascertain if she's following along in class. I know it's still early on, but if she is reading at this level, then I will need to adjust my lesson plans for her."

"She's still not talking to you?" Hannah turned and regarded her daughter, nose in book, unaware of the world around her.

"Not a word, aside from registration in the morning when she says she's here. I don't want to push her too much, but…" Miss Spencer sighed. "I can't confirm she is reading these books. Obviously, you say she is, but I need her to speak to me to confirm that."

Hannah knew there was an easy way to solve this matter and allow her and Rosie out of the room. She nodded and turned to look at Rosie.

"Pumpkin? Can you come here a minute?"

Rosie put her bookmark in her book and walked over. Hannah lifted her into her lap and wrapped her arms around her.

"What do you need to know?" Hannah asked Miss Spencer.

She grabbed a book from her desk and handed it over. "Could Rosie read some of this out loud?"

"Sure." Hannah opened the book to a random page and held it opened in front of Rosie. "Can you read some of this for us, please, pumpkin?"

Rosie nodded happily and started reading. Hannah knew that Rosie's courage soared as long as she was nearby. She felt proud that her daughter felt so safe and secure in the knowledge that her mum would always protect her.

She looked up at Miss Spencer who was staring at Rosie with fascination. Hannah knew that Rosie's reading was good. Of course, it would be as she did it all the time.

"Thank you, Rosie," Miss Spencer interrupted her reading after a couple of paragraphs. "That was very good indeed."

Hannah closed the book and put it back on the desk.

"Rosie, do you know your alphabet?" Miss Spencer asked.

Rosie nodded.

"You'll have to say it out loud," Hannah whispered in her ear.

Rosie reeled off the alphabet without hesitation.

"That's very good," Miss Spencer said. "Did Mummy teach you that?"

"No, YouTube," Rosie replied.

Hannah chuckled. "With my supervision. Obviously, she's not had free reign on YouTube."

Miss Spencer smiled. "Rosie, what day is it?"

"Wednesday," Rosie asked.

"And can you spell Wednesday?"

"W-E-D-N-E-S-D-A-Y."

Miss Spencer looked up at Hannah. "Has Rosie attended education prior to starting here? My notes say that she wasn't in Reception."

"No, she's never been in school before," Hannah said. "As I said, she's always been bright."

Miss Spencer leaned back in her chair and regarded them for a few moments. She opened her desk drawer and started looking through bits of paper.

"Rosie, how would you like to have a look at an exam paper? You can take it home with you and see if you can answer any of the questions. No pressure, just for fun. I can give you one about English, so spelling and reading. And one about maths. How does that sound?"

Rosie sat up with interest. "Yes, please."

"It's not an official exam, but it is an old exam paper. You can have a look and see how much you can answer. If you can't answer them, then that's nothing to worry about. It's just for fun. But you can't ask YouTube. Or Mummy."

Rosie giggled. "Mummy is rubbish at numbers and spelling."

Hannah felt her cheeks heat up in a blush. "It's true, she gets none of her academic talents from me."

"I'm sure she gets other talents from you," Miss Spencer said, that distracting smile back on her face.

In another lifetime, Hannah would have happily

pursued someone like Miss Spencer. If this were six years ago in a bar, it would be a different matter entirely. She would have bought her a drink, casually chatted, and fished for some information. Sure, she was older, but Hannah had always found maturity sexy in a woman.

Rosie shifted in her lap, reminding her that this wasn't six years ago in a bar. It was now, in a school, with her daughter in her lap and her daughter's teacher sliding two exam papers across the desk.

"In your own time, no hurry," Miss Spencer was saying. "And, again, it doesn't matter if you can't answer them."

"Can I do them now, Mummy?" Rosie asked her.

"You can do them when we go and see Uncle Adrian." She didn't want to mention the salon, in case Miss Spencer thought that wasn't an appropriate place for a child to spend her afternoons.

"Yay!" Rosie jumped off her lap and grabbed the papers. She dashed over to get her bag.

"Well, that's made her evening," Hannah said. "Thank you."

"No, thank you, it's nice to hear her talking. You have a wonderful daughter."

"I do," Hannah agreed. She turned to watch Rosie packing her things away, anything to stop herself from getting lost in Miss Spencer's eyes. It was only the second time they'd met, and Hannah was already finding herself intrigued by Miss Spencer. It had to stop, she decided.

She glanced over at the desktop, noting there was no ring on Miss Spencer's finger.

She snapped her head back towards Rosie. *Stop it,* she told herself.

Another evening had disappeared in a blur. Rosie had spent the afternoon in the staff room at Chopz, had a quick dinner, then a shower, and went straight into bed. Well, not straight into bed. She had spent a few minutes complaining about her bedtime again, but soon drifted off in the midst of arguing.

Hannah had taken that as a win.

She cleaned the kitchen and made Rosie's lunch for the next day. Thoughts of Miss Spencer floated around her mind. The woman was unfairly attractive, and with Rosie's exams suggesting the need for a second meeting, any hope she had had of not seeing her daughter's teacher had flown out of the window.

Of course, she knew that her daughter was talented. She had an insatiable curiosity and a thirst for knowledge like she had never seen before. Hannah had indulged it as much as she could. It had quickly become apparent that Rosie could take to any new subject, easily learning things that were often beyond Hannah's understanding with the help of some books from the library or a quick search on the Internet.

She'd never been academically minded, and her maths skills had always been atrocious. Rosie took to numbers, though, like a duck to water. It had been a weird sensation when her five-year-old daughter had first explained to her an easier way to do her monthly banking.

Rosie was five going on fifty in many ways, and that worried Hannah. She wanted Rosie to have a normal childhood. To play, to make friends, to do what five-year-olds did. But that was already looking like it wasn't going to happen.

After all, Miss Spencer had quickly picked up on Rosie's abilities.

Hannah was proud of Rosie. Who wouldn't be? But she secretly wished that Rosie didn't have to stand out. Blending into the crowd was all she had ever wanted when she was a child, and it was the thing she wanted most for Rosie. People who blended into the crowd were left alone. People who stood out were bullied. The thought of Rosie being bullied made her heart ache.

She looked at the completed exam papers on the dining table. She'd tried to ignore them, but she couldn't. Her daughter had breezed through examination papers in English and Maths labelled "Key Stage One." Hannah knew these were the tests that Rosie should be taking when she was seven.

She flipped through the pages. Most of the questions were answered, with a few left blank. When she read the questions that Rosie had skipped, she realised she couldn't answer them either.

She put the papers into Rosie's bag with a sigh.

This could be a problem, she thought to herself.

THIS ENDS NOW

"ARE YOU OKAY, MUMMY?" Rosie asked.

Hannah squeezed her hand and looked down at Rosie's concerned eyes.

"I'm fine. I didn't sleep very well, so I'm very tired. In fact, I might fall asleep… right here." Hannah stopped in the middle of the pavement, closed her eyes, and lowered her head.

Rosie shook her hand. "Mummy, you're not asleep."

"Give me another minute, and I might be," Hannah muttered.

She opened her eyes and offered Rosie a quick smile and a wink. They continued the walk towards the school.

Hannah was exhausted. Stress dreams had woken her up every couple of hours throughout the night. They all had the same theme: Rosie being bullied or in some way excluded. In one, Rosie's brain had grown to ten times its usual size, and she was in a laboratory while Miss Spencer performed tests on her.

It had been ridiculous, but Hannah knew the absurd dreams were pulled straight from her fears.

Ever since Hannah had learned she was pregnant, she was determined that her child would never have a school experience like hers. While her own situation had been caused out of neglect and bullying, she wondered if Rosie's exceptional intelligence was going to lead her down the same path.

Children, specifically bullies, focused on peers who were different. Standing out in school was bad. Hannah had already been concerned that Rosie wouldn't be able to make friends because she was shy. Now Miss Spencer wanted to add to the complicated situation by having Rosie complete tests for seven-year-olds.

It wasn't happening. Hannah had made that decision at three o'clock in the morning. Miss Spencer could put any ideas of personally mentoring the next Einstein out of her mind. Rosie was going to have a completely normal school experience.

"You're coming in?" Rosie looked at her in confusion as they both crossed the threshold onto the school property.

"I'm going to give your exam papers to Miss Spencer," Hannah explained. "Just to make sure she gets them and knows you didn't cheat."

She hated lying to Rosie, but she was too young to understand the implications of what was happening. She'd had fun with the tests, but what came next wouldn't be fun.

Hannah unclipped the clasps on the rucksack and took the exam papers out of the bag, rolling them up so the other eagle-eyed parents wouldn't notice them. She bent down and kissed Rosie's hair.

"I'll take these upstairs to Miss Spencer. I might not see you before the bell goes, so have a good day at school. I'll see you this afternoon."

"Okay." Rosie's eyes were already scanning the playground, looking for her friends.

Hannah hurried towards the school before she lost her nerve. Seeing Miss Spencer was enough to put her on edge but saying what she was about to say made it worse.

Guarding the door was Lucy Gibson.

Hannah kept a neutral face as best she could. "Lucy."

"Hannah." Lucy took a tiny step to the side to let her past.

Hannah brushed past her. She hurried up the steps, taking them two at a time. She walked down the corridor in a daze, sleep-deprived and eager to have her encounter over with as soon as possible.

The form room's door was open, and Miss Spencer was sat at her desk. Eating an apple of all things. The woman was straight out of a movie, one in which the sexy, older teacher read the morning paper with her glasses perched on the end of her nose while casually biting into the juicy flesh of an apple.

Hannah took a small suck of air and marched into the room. She tried to place the exam papers down gently on the desk, but the force shocked Miss Spencer into jumping in her seat.

"She's done them," Hannah said, "but that's it. I don't want any special treatment. Nothing. She's a little girl, a normal five-year-old and she'll do normal five-year-old work. Okay? This ends now. No more… exams… or… or anything."

Nerves were making her lose her pre-prepared speech. She nodded her head sharply and left before Miss Spencer could reply.

Hannah wrapped her hands around her coffee mug. She'd been pacing the staff room in Chopz for the last thirty minutes while she told Adrian exactly how deluded Rosie's teacher was.

"I told her no way," Hannah repeated. "Not happening. Not to my little girl."

"Hmm," Adrian said. He'd been sitting, watching her pace since she started ranting.

"I'm right, aren't I?" she demanded.

"If you say so."

She stopped and stared at him. "What's that supposed to mean?"

"If you say so." Adrian shrugged.

"No, if you have something to say, say it."

"I really don't want to," he confessed. "You're scary when you get like this. I know you think you're protecting Rosie but—"

"THINK? I AM protecting her!" Hannah argued.

"See? Scary."

Hannah put her mug on the table, probably with a little too much intensity. She pulled out a chair and sat down, looking at Adrian intently.

"Okay, I promise to remain quiet and you can tell me what you really think. Because you clearly disagree."

"I don't have a death wish," Adrian pointed out. "I'm fine nodding when you think I should nod."

"But I *know* you don't agree with me. Come on. Tell me what you think." Hannah folded her arms and leaned back in her chair. She was convinced that she was right, but if Adrian had something to say, she'd listen. And correct him, if necessary.

He blew out a long breath and looked at the table top, presumably to avoid her intense stare.

"Rosie is great. You know I love her like she's my own kid," he started. "But she's not a normal kid. She cashed up the till in the salon when she was four. Four, Han, *four*. That isn't normal. She's been reading, counting, adding, and doing all those things way early for her age. She's obviously got a photographic memory, but she can also *process* what she is reading and that's incredible."

"I'm not denying that," Hannah said.

"You kinda are. You tell people she's bright. It's a massive understatement. She's amazing. And, the only reason you are keeping it on the down-low is because you don't want her to be treated different. I get it, really, I do. I know you had a shit time at school. And I know you don't want that for Rosie, but what if you're holding her back?"

Hannah opened her mouth to argue, but he held up his hand and fixed her with a pleading look.

"I think you're projecting," he said. "All you wanted to do when you were at school was fit in. You wanted to be normal, end of story. Maybe Rosie doesn't feel that way?

Maybe Rosie isn't you? Maybe Rosie is happy about a chance to reach her full potential?"

Hannah swallowed down some choice words.

"This teacher, Miss Spencer? She does this for a living. She's spotted that Rosie is really clever, and she's trying to see how clever so she can give her the best possible opportunities in her education. I know you think she'll make Rosie stand out, but maybe she won't. You haven't given her a chance to talk it through. You're not giving her a chance to do her job."

He swiped his empty coffee mug from the table and crossed to the machine on the counter, pouring a fresh cup.

"How many people come in here and try to tell you how hair works? How many people with completely white hair have told you they want to be a dark brunette? Or a dark brunette that wants to be platinum blonde? How many times have you had to have the conversation about shades and explain how hair works?"

"Hundreds," she admitted.

"And you're the expert. People come in with no idea, and we complain about how they don't trust us, the experts. Miss Spencer, she's the expert. You're Rosie's mum, and your job is to love her, protect her, and give her everything she needs. Miss Spencer, she's her teacher. Let her do that job. At the very least, speak to Rosie. She's wiser than any of us. Let her decide. Maybe she'd rather learn about nuclear physics than have any friends. It's her choice, Han."

Hannah wanted to argue, but she couldn't. All her denials dried up in her throat.

"I know why you want to keep her where she is, and I totally get that you think you're doing the right thing, but I think you need to really be sure. You don't want to throw away a chance for Rosie just because you had a bad time at school." Adrian gestured towards the door with his mug. "I better get set up for Mr Jensen. He'll be here in a few minutes. Are you okay?"

She nodded. "Yeah, I'm okay. Thanks for being honest. I needed to hear that."

"You know I'm here for you. And Rosie. Whatever you need."

She looked up at him, blinking away the tears that threatened to fall. "I appreciate that. More than you know."

He smiled softly and left the staff room. She closed her eyes and flopped forward onto the table. *I knew being a mum would be hard, but why is it this hard?*

ROUND TWO

ALICE LOOKED AT THE TALL, rickety wooden ladder suspiciously.

"It's safe, right?" she asked.

The school caretaker, Jim, nodded quickly. "Had it for fifty years. Never had a problem. Not like these new metal ones."

She'd bitten the bullet and decided to give the room a lick of magnolia paint herself. She'd been at the local hardware store, purchasing items for her new house, when a multi-buy deal on large decorator pots of paint had spurred her on.

It wasn't until she got the paint to the school and asked Jim to help her carry it to her form room's storage cupboard that she'd thought about the high Victorian ceilings. They were at least three meters high, well beyond the average set of domestic steps.

Jim in turn had offered his ladder, but not his assistance.

He was seventy and refused to allow her to carry the

paint from her car to the classroom. But helping her to paint wasn't mentioned, even though she suspected it was somewhere in his job description.

She'd gotten used to Willows School's lethargy when it came to change and improvement. Hardaker's attitude had infected everyone. No one seemed to see a problem with the crumbling building, and no one agreed with her that a better working environment would benefit the children.

Still, no one was standing in her way, so she would do it herself and prove them all wrong. She'd brought some old clothes in and had gotten changed as soon as school had finished for the day. Now she had brushes, rollers, paint, Jim's ladder, and sheer terror at the prospect of using it.

"If that's it then, Miss Spencer?" Jim asked, itching to go home.

"Yes, thank you for your help."

"Good luck," he said as he left.

She looked at the ladder again and shivered nervously. She hated heights with a passion, and now she was about to climb a fifty-year-old wooden ladder in order to paint her classroom. If her ex-colleagues from the city could see her now.

She took a deep breath and forced herself to get on with it. Natural daylight wouldn't be around much longer, and the lights in the building were unreliable at best. The last thing she needed was to be stuck up the ladder when the lights went out.

Jim had also kindly lent her a smaller pot for the paint. She poured some from the bigger pot into the smaller container and put a paint brush into the thick liquid.

There was no more delaying it.

She looked up at the ladder and swallowed.

She climbed slowly, leaning her weight forward, clutching the ladders with one hand, and balancing the smaller paint pot with the other.

"Fucking place," she mumbled under her breath.

Eventually, she arrived at the top of the ladder. She focused on the wall, refusing to look down. She adjusted her position, took the paintbrush in her right hand, and shakily leant forward to apply some paint the wall.

"It will all be worth it," she reminded herself.

The wall thirstily sucked up the paint. It took several applications before the paint started to cover, and she'd only managed to do an area thirty centimetres square in what felt like several hours because of her pounding heart.

She heard a cough and turned her head. Hannah Hall stood in the doorway, looking up at her.

As if the evening couldn't get any more pleasant. *Oh great, is this round two?* she wondered.

"Hi, can I talk to you?" Hannah asked.

Alice breathed in and then out deeply. She didn't know if she'd get back up the ladder once she got back down to solid ground, but she couldn't have a conversation with a parent while up a ladder.

"Of course, one moment," she said.

She rebalanced the paint pot and slowly made her way down. Her hands shook, and she had a mental image of falling and breaking her neck. At least someone would be there to dial 999. After what seemed like an age, she touched a shaky foot to the wooden floor.

"Sorry," she apologised, "I'm not good with heights."

"I can tell," Hannah said. "Should a teacher be painting the classroom? Isn't that Old Jim's job?"

"Old Jim draws the line at providing equipment," Alice explained, pointing to the ladder. "I told him I had a fear of heights, and he recommended facing my fears."

"How's that going?" Hannah asked with a disarming grin.

"I'm still terrified I'm going to die."

"I wonder what he'd suggest if you were scared of spiders?"

Alice shivered and held up her hand. "Please."

"Oh, you are? Forget I mentioned anything. Any other fears I should avoid talking about?"

"Let's see, spiders, snakes, heights, the dark, fire… most things, really," Alice put the paint pot down and wiped her hands on a rag. "I'm a bit of a coward."

"You're not, I just saw you up that ladder," Hannah said.

Alice rolled her shoulders. "Necessity. Anyway, can I help you?"

Hannah clasped her hands in front of her and looked at the floor for a moment. "I wanted to apologise for this morning. I was rude. And wrong. I didn't have the best time in school, and I didn't want Rosie to have the rough time I had."

Alice felt the tension leave her shoulders. It wasn't a second round, thank goodness.

"That's quite all right, I understand." She gestured for Hannah to take a seat. "I looked at the papers. Rosie demolished the Key Stage One tests. The only questions she struggled with were the ones where the phrasing was something she probably wasn't familiar with. I'm sure she knew the answers, but not the way that part of the curriculum is taught."

Hannah nodded her understanding. Her shoulders were tight, and her eyes looked panicked. "So, what now?"

"Well, Rosie should take the Key Stage One test in two years, but she's already beyond that. In fact, I suspect she is even beyond Key Stage Two. But I won't know without further tests. Rosie is still very shy and not communicating much in class. Definitely not with me. I'd love to find out more about her academic skills, but I don't want to push her or upset her. And I certainly don't want to single her out from the rest of the group."

She noticed Hannah's shoulders lower, but there was still a tension surrounding her.

"I've worked with gifted children before," Alice explained. "If they are not nurtured and given the correct education and challenges, they can become bored. Sometimes that leads to them becoming angry or even depressed."

Hannah's expression changed from guarded to concerned. "What do you recommend?" she asked.

"I'd like to test Rosie and see what her level of education is at present, what gaps there are, and work out a plan for her."

Hannah bit her lip and looked away for a moment. Alice regarded her. It was obvious that Rosie was her world. Not that any parent didn't feel that way about their child, but it seemed more evident with Hannah.

"Okay. But only if Rosie agrees. I know that sounds

crazy, but she knows her own mind. I think you should ask her, she likes you."

Alice blinked. "Does she?"

"Yep. At home it's, 'Miss Spencer says this, Miss Spencer says that' all night." Hannah chuckled. "I'm sick of you," she said with a wink.

"Apologies." Alice smiled playfully. "I'd happily talk to her, but she seems painfully shy around me. Unless you are there. Would you be willing to come in after school one night? I'm sure she'll be much more comfortable if you are there with her."

Hannah nodded. "Yeah, sure. We can't do tomorrow as we're going swimming after school. Monday would be best."

"Monday sounds great. Thank you. I know it's a lot to take on, but Rosie is an exceptional child and I want to ensure that she gets the best care and education possible. I've seen children's personalities change when they become bored with their schoolwork, either because it's too simple or too advanced for them. I just want the best for you and Rosie."

Hannah stood up and stuck her hands into her jean's pockets. "Rosie is my everything. I just want her to be happy. I'm sorry I overreacted this morning. As I say, bad memories of this place."

Alice wanted to ask about this, but got the impression that Hannah wasn't ready to talk. She knew that their parent-teacher relationship needed a little more time and nurturing before she could be that bold.

"Think nothing of it," she said. "Water under the bridge."

"Thank you." Hannah smiled, and Alice had to break eye contact before she got too lost in those soulful eyes.

"So, I'll see you on Monday. Unless I see you before, in the playground," she said, attempting to draw the conversation to a close. She knew she was blushing and didn't want to embarrass herself any further in front of Ms Hall.

"Cool. Good luck with the painting." Hannah nodded towards the death-trap ladder.

"Thank you, goodnight." She waved.

"Night." Hannah grinned at Alice's waving hand before walking away.

Alice stared angrily at her hand, wondering what the traitorous appendage was thinking. She rolled her eyes, shook her head, and forced herself to return to the ladder.

13

COLIN STRIKES

ALICE ENJOYED the warmth of the sun on her face. September was squeezing out a last burst of pleasant weather before autumn took hold. It was still a little windy, but Alice was determined to soak up a little more vitamin D while on playground duty.

Lucy Gibson joined her again, and while Alice was glad of the company, she had gotten the distinct impression that Lucy was an unstoppable gossip. Even as the children ran around them, Lucy continued telling her the story of a local supermarket worker being caught in a compromising position with a delivery driver.

Alice had no interest in the tale. Nor in any other tales about the residents of Fairlight.

She tried to distract Lucy from her narrative or look like she was uninterested, but Lucy continued on regardless. Alice didn't want to be rude, and it was nice to have a friend. Or something resembling one. So, she tilted her face slightly towards the winter sun and counted down the minutes until the afternoon break was over.

A scream echoed out across the playground.

The first thing Alice had learnt as a teacher was to distinguish between real screams and play screams. Children loved to shout, and girls in particular were never shy of showcasing their impressions of a murder victim. The first few weeks of her teaching career had been filled with Alice assuming someone was horribly injured only to find that an innocent game of chase was being played.

But that was a long time ago and Alice could easily identify a real scream now. She turned and headed toward the sound without a second thought.

A group had gathered, another indication that something serious was going on.

"Let me through," she commanded as she eased children out of the way.

In the middle of the crowd she was completely unsurprised to see Colin. He was still too young to have mastered the ability to look innocent or to try to blend into the crowd. Instead, he was standing over someone and looking every bit the bully she knew he was.

On the ground was Rosie Hall, tears running down her face.

Alice took a breath, trying to contain the anger she felt bubbling up inside her.

"Colin, go to Mr Hardaker," she said, even though she knew it was a pointless exercise. It was the only thing she could do. Sending a child to the headmaster would usually set in motion a chain of events that would stop the behaviour, but when the headmaster was as laid-back as Mr Hardaker, nothing was likely to change.

"Nothing to see here," she told the children who had

gathered around. Being nosey seemed to be genetic in Fairlight.

She crouched down and looked Rosie over. There was a nasty-looking scratch on the girl's temple. "Are you okay?"

Rosie nodded, even though it was painfully clear that she wasn't.

"Can you stand up?"

Again, Rosie nodded. Alice held out her hand and helped guide her to her feet, brushing dried leaves and dirt off of her uniform as she did.

She noticed that some of the gawking children had yet to disperse. She looked up at them, and they soon scattered at her glare.

She looked back at Rosie and saw more tears fall down her cheeks and a quivering bottom lip.

"Let's get you to the school nurse," Alice suggested. "You'll be as good as new in no time."

Rosie held out her arms shakily. Alice realised then that Rosie wasn't going to be able to walk herself into the school, not because she was injured but she because she was so shaken up.

It wasn't normal procedure to carry a child to nurse's office, but it wasn't explicitly forbidden either. Not to mention that fact that Rosie was tiny, and Alice knew she could easily carry her.

And knew that she would.

Rosie desperately needed comfort. She may not have spoken with Alice much during class, but she was now reaching out to her.

Literally.

Alice heard Lucy speaking with Colin, getting his version of events and preparing to accompany him to the headmaster's office. *Good, she can deal with him,* she thought.

She reached out, pulled Rosie into her arms, and stood up easily. She was lucky that Rosie was a five-year-old that weighed next to nothing.

Lucy gave her a nod as she passed by, confirming that she would deal with everything and Alice was to check Rosie was okay.

Rosie's arms wrapped around her neck, and Alice quickly walked her to the nurse's office. She was fairly certain that Rosie hadn't sustained any real injuries aside from the scratch on her forehead, but she was still anxious to be positive of the fact.

Why in heaven's name had Colin pushed the quiet girl over? She knew that bullies seldom had good reasons and that now wasn't the time to ask. She'd need to get both sides of the story, but she needed Rosie to be in a better state when she started prodding.

The nurse was just finishing patching up a scraped knee when they entered the small room. Alice placed Rosie on the edge of the medical bed. The student with the scraped knee was sent on their way, and the nurse, Brenda, turned to Rosie.

Alice stood back and allowed the woman to do her work. Questions were asked, appendages were moved, and it was concluded that the cut above the right eyebrow and a bruised bottom were the only injuries.

The nurse doused a ball of cotton wool in some kind

of cleansing liquid and approached Rosie, who quickly flinched back and hid her face.

"We need to clean that wound," she said, bedside manner presumably having been lost in between the countless scrapes and cuts that passed through the small room on a daily basis.

Rosie shook her head.

Brenda made another attempt, and Rosie pushed herself further away.

"Maybe I can try?" Alice offered, hating to see Rosie being tormented by the well-meaning nurse.

"If you like," Brenda said, she gestured her head towards the plastic gloves. "Cotton wool balls and plasters are in that cupboard."

Alice pulled out two gloves and snapped them onto her hands. Brenda was already walking out of the room to give them more space. Alice wondered if the disenfranchised mood came after working at Willows for too long, or if people who felt that way were drawn to the school like moths to a flame.

She got a fresh cotton wool ball and put an antibacterial solution on it.

"May I?" She gestured toward Rosie's cut.

Rosie regarded her for a couple of seconds. She slowly shuffled her way back to a sitting position on the edge of the bed.

Alice approached slowly. She held Rosie's chin in one hand and ever so gently started to clean the wound with the cotton wool.

"Is that okay?"

"Yes," Rosie said softly.

"What happened?" Alice asked, trying to get information and distract Rosie from any pain at the same time.

"Colin pushed me over," Rosie said.

"Why did he do that?"

"He said my mummy is a lesbian, and then he pushed me."

Alice paused for a moment. She wondered if it was true. Was Hannah a lesbian? Or was it just the worst insult an immature mind like Colin's could produce? She certainly wasn't about to ask Rosie.

"He said that his daddy said that my mummy was a lesbian. He's mean, and I don't want to go back to class. I don't want to see him ever again," Rosie said.

Satisfied the wound was clean, Alice dropped the used cotton wool into the bin and picked up a sticking plaster to cover the cut.

"I understand why you feel that way," Alice agreed, "but if you do that, then you let the bully win. You like school, and if you stay away from class then you would be letting Colin take away something that you enjoy. And that's not fair, is it?"

"No. But I won't want to see him."

"I wish I could make that happen, but you live in the same small town and you go to the same school. You'll definitely see him again, no matter how hard you try," Alice said. "A better solution might be for you and me to speak to him and explain that what he said was mean. You'll be surprised how cowardly bullies are when confronted."

She applied the plaster, softly pressing down its edges.

"Really?" Rosie asked, seeming doubtful.

"Really," Alice confirmed. "Because bullies are the biggest cowards of them all. The only way they can make themselves feel good is to pull other people down. And it's up to people like you to tell them that that isn't a nice thing to do."

"I don't know if I want to," Rosie confessed.

"What if I help you? What if I make sure that Colin apologises?"

Rosie mulled the thought over for a few moments before finally nodding her head.

"Good," Alice said. "How does that feel?" She indicated the plaster on Rosie's forehead.

"All better," Rosie said.

Alice smiled. She wished all injuries could be healed by a measure of distraction and the feel of safety. Obviously, Rosie's cut hadn't vanished, but the youngster felt as if it had. That was enough.

Her thoughts turned to Colin Whittaker, how she would attempt to speak to him and get him to understand that his behaviour was wrong. It was usually a job for the headmaster, but Alice knew that she'd have to take it on. Much the same as the decorating. She wondered what other tasks outside of her remit she would end up taking on.

She looked at Rosie's smiling face, though, and knew in that second that she'd do anything to keep her students safe and happy and looking at her in the way Rosie was doing right then.

14

STEVE THE BRICK

IF HANNAH HADN'T BEEN so angry and frightened, she would have marvelled at her ability to race through so many emotions in such a short space of time. When she'd stepped through the dreaded school gates, she'd quickly encountered excitement, confusion, concern, fear, and, finally, fury.

Seeing Rosie on the school step, her hand in Miss Spencer's, had been intriguing. Right up until she noticed the sticking plaster on her daughter's forehead and the nervous look on Miss Spencer's face.

She'd jogged across the playground, kneeling in front of Rosie and checking her over for any other injuries.

"What happened?" she demanded.

"There was a slight altercation in the playground this afternoon," Miss Spencer explained calmly. "I assure you that Rosie is fine. I just wanted to explain it to you myself."

"Altercation?" Hannah blinked. "You mean a fight."

"No, not a fight," Miss Spencer replied quickly.

"Colin pushed me, and I fell," Rosie explained.

Hannah felt the breath leave her lungs. Colin. The little bastard. She reminded herself that it was wrong to murder children, and probably frowned upon to give them a solid kick in the shins.

"He… he pushed you?" She couldn't understand why Colin would react that way. What could Rosie possibly have done to upset him?

Rosie nodded. Hannah glanced down and noticed a bruise on her daughter's knee. She started checking her over more thoroughly for any other injuries.

"It's okay, Miss Spencer made him apologise to me," Rosie continued. "In front of the whole class."

Hannah looked at Rosie's face. She seemed okay. The public apology had obviously cheered her up, but Hannah was still fresh to the situation, reeling from the news that someone had pushed her baby girl down.

"Why did he push you? I don't understand."

"He said that you were a lesbian," Rosie said.

Hannah bit her lip and looked down at the stone step Rosie stood on. She'd always been open and honest with Rosie about her sexuality. She wanted her daughter to grow up with an understanding and appreciation that all people were different, and that those differences were to be celebrated and not hidden. But children like Colin, and no doubt Colin's parents whom she classified as children, didn't feel that way.

Rosie being the victim of bullying was her worst nightmare. Her being the reason for that bullying was the icing on the nightmare cake.

"Kids can be cruel, especially about things they don't

understand," Miss Spencer said softly. "But I had a long conversation with Colin this afternoon, and I can assure you that this won't be repeated."

Hannah stood shakily. Rosie looked fine. Kids bounced back a lot easier than adults most of the time. Meanwhile, she knew it would take some time for her to come to terms with the fact that her sexuality had caused her daughter problems at school.

"Mummy, I don't want to go swimming tonight. My plaster might fall off." Rosie gestured to her forehead with the hand that wasn't tightly fastened to Miss Spencer's.

"It's a small graze, but I felt it best to keep it clean," Miss Spencer added.

Hannah nodded distractedly. She wasn't too concerned about Rosie's injuries, she trusted Miss Spencer. If there was something more serious, then she would have noticed and informed her of it. It seemed to be a case of a graze, a bruise or two, and a shaken little girl. Her goal now was to soothe Rosie and make sure she had a nice evening to replace the memories of the upsetting afternoon.

Her daughter was still clutching Miss Spencer's hand. Hannah hoped this meant that there was a small silver lining: they had finally had a breakthrough and Rosie was now more comfortable with her teacher.

An idea formed in her mind.

"Seems we have a free evening," Hannah said. She looked at Miss Spencer and raised her eyebrow.

Miss Spencer looked at her for a moment before the penny seemed to drop.

"Oh, I'm free this evening, too."

Hannah looked down at Rosie.

"Pumpkin, Miss Spencer spoke to me earlier about giving you some more tests and answering some questions to see just how big that big brain of yours is. What do you think? Would you like to do that?"

She already knew Rosie would love the idea. Tests and questions were like sugar to Rosie.

The girl looked from her teacher to her mother with excitement in her eyes. "Really?"

"Really," Hannah confirmed.

"I'd love to ask you some questions if you feel up to it," Miss Spencer asked. "I think you're finding your schoolwork a little too easy. I need to find something that you'll find a bit more challenging."

"What do you think?" Hannah asked. "I can't believe I'm asking a child of mine this, but do you want to spend a couple more hours in school?"

Rosie nodded so hard her head nearly fell off.

"Wonderful." Miss Spencer smiled, and Hannah couldn't help but smile back.

She watched as teacher and student turned and entered the building. She took a much-needed deep breath and a moment to gather her thoughts before following them.

Hannah was bored. Obviously, she wanted to support her daughter's education, but she could only look interested in schoolwork for so long before her true feelings on the matter shone through.

They were back in the form room. Miss Spencer was

sitting beside Rosie at her desk, guiding her through workbooks and exercise sheets in a soft tone. Hannah had taken a seat near them and tried to follow along, but it hadn't been long before boredom set in.

She'd always half-heartedly wondered if she had some form of attention deficit disorder. Paying attention to anything was a struggle. Trying to remain focused on something she found dull was actually impossible.

While the subject matter was tedious, the person behind it was not. It was clear to see that Miss Spencer was brilliant with Rosie. She offered her encouragement and praise where necessary, giving her a slight clue or push at the right moments.

When Hannah became a mother, she had discovered something very interesting about the people around her. Some were naturally good at speaking to children, and some... were not. Most people had good intentions, but some were just not good with children at all. Some spoke down to Rosie, as if she were a baby even when she was old enough to tie her own shoes. Some asked her silly questions, and some tried to avoid talking to her altogether.

It wasn't something she'd ever noticed before, but it became clear that some people had a way with children and some people didn't. Miss Spencer absolutely did. Not just because she was a teacher, it seemed ingrained in her. She seemed to be naturally good with people, able to read a room or a situation and respond to it well.

Rosie hung off her every word, soaking up any praise and nodding along as explanations were given.

While Miss Spencer was occupied with her student,

Hannah took in her side profile. Her hair was tucked behind her ear, and her skin crinkled at her eye as she focused. Her smile and laugh were infectious.

Too infectious.

Hannah blinked a few times and looked away. Now was not the time to be having impure thoughts, or any thoughts, about her daughter's teacher. Her eyes drifted towards the corner of the room that had recently been painted. A snigger left her lips without permission.

"Something amusing about my decorating skills?" Miss Spencer asked.

"Yes, they're terrible," Hannah replied honestly.

"It's not my fault the walls haven't seen any moisture for so long that they are soaking up all the paint."

Hannah got up and walked over to the wall to inspect it more closely. She turned back to look at Miss Spencer, who was watching her with an amused smile.

"Terrible. I'm going to have to give you a one-star review on Google Maps," Hannah said seriously.

"Only one? I did manage to get some paint on."

Hannah tsked and shook her head. She looked down at the paint pots and brushes which had been left in the corner, hidden away from the children.

"May I?"

"Oh, no, that's not necessary. Really," Miss Spencer said. "I wouldn't want you to ruin your clothes."

"I'll be careful. And I'd like to do something. I'm not much help with what you're doing, and this will keep me occupied."

"Mummy gets bored easily," Rosie added without looking up from her work.

"Thanks, sweetie," Hannah said with a shake of her head.

Miss Spencer looked amused. Her lips curled into yet another dazzling smile, and Hannah hurried to distract herself with the paint supplies.

Before long she had set up a dust sheet and was happily applying paint to the crumbling wall as she listened to the soft sounds of Rosie and Miss Spencer talking about verbs and multiplication. It was strangely nice. Hannah hadn't thought she'd experience anything other than misery at Willows School, but now she found herself carefully applying paint to the wall of her old form room.

Below her calm exterior, fury still bubbled away that someone had assaulted her sweet, tiny daughter. Because of *her*. She knew there was nothing she could do. The moment had passed, it had been dealt with, and Rosie was on her way to forgetting about it. But the fact that it had happened at all, and the knowledge that it might happen again, ate at her.

She didn't know why her sexuality was a topic of conversation for Fairlight. It wasn't like she was dating anyone. Okay, she had dated before Rosie came along. And she'd had the most poorly thought out relationship ever while she was in the early stages of pregnancy. Pregnancy brain and the shock of impending motherhood had sent her to a lesbian bar in the nearest city with a friend. Abi had been drunk, but Hannah had been sober and should have known better. They'd dated for a month. It had been loud, messy, and very public.

"Is that brick in particular your favourite?"

Miss Spencer's rich voice pulled her back to the present. She realised she'd been painting the same three square inches for some time.

"Yes. I call him Steve," she replied.

"Oh, have you named all the bricks?"

"Of course, classes were long and dull, what else was I to do?" Hannah winked. She noticed that Rosie was nowhere in sight and realised that her little trip down memory lane had been a more absorbing than she'd thought.

"She's popped to the bathroom. We're all done," Miss Spencer answered her questioning look.

"Dare I ask?" Hannah held her breath, awaiting the judgement on her daughter's future education. She knew most parents would be besides themselves with joy to find out that their child had exceptional skills and tried to keep that in mind.

"She's… gifted. Very gifted. I have a lot to review within the paperwork we've just completed. There are gaps in her knowledge, but they stem more from learning the correct processes rather than the base knowledge."

"You've lost me," Hannah confessed.

"When we attend school, we don't just learn facts and figures, we learn how to reach conclusions and the manner in which to solve equations. Rosie can read very well, she can retain knowledge—I suspect a photographic memory is at play—and her math skills are incredible. But she struggles when presented with a problem that she doesn't know how to solve because she's never been taught the process."

"That makes sense. So, what now?"

"I'll develop a new lesson plan for her. It's not as easy as saying she is at a certain point in the curriculum. I wouldn't want her to skip ahead and miss out on key foundational things. It's about identifying what she knows, what she needs to learn, and the best way to teach her. She's way ahead of the rest of her class, and even if they were learning the same thing at the same time, she would catch on much faster."

Hannah felt a sinking feeling. A different lesson plan, skipping ahead. Neither of these things were going to help Rosie make friends with her classmates.

Miss Spencer looked nervously towards the door and then back towards Hannah. She wrung her hands together and licked her lips.

"Um, I wanted to ask… Considering what, well, what was said. That is to say, what I know, even though it wasn't directly said to me, but we can't put the bolted horse back in the stable… I was wondering if you'd, well, if you'd like to go for a drink? I mean, with me. A drink with me. If you'd like. I mean, I don't know if you're seeing anyone. If you are, then I'm sorry, but—"

"I'm not seeing anyone," Hannah said, cutting off the woman's adorable, nervous rambling. "I don't really get much time to go out for a drink, though."

Miss Spencer's face fell. "Of course, of course, that was a stupid thing to say. You're a mother, of course you don't exactly get a lot of time off. I'm sorry, I shouldn't have asked."

Hannah realised that her words sounded like a brush-off. A polite thanks, but no thanks. It was an opportunity to leave it there, to go no further, but her words hadn't been a no. In fact, for a brief second, she'd actually considered the logistics of going out for a drink with the woman.

Dating was supposed to be very firmly off the table. But there was something about this woman that drew Hannah to her.

"How about dinner instead? You could come over to my place." The words were out of Hannah's mouth before she had a chance to stop herself.

Miss Spencer's face morphed from embarrassment to delight in a split second. "That sounds wonderful, but I wouldn't want to impose."

"You won't. We'd love to have you. You're Rosie's new favourite person."

Her smile could guide ships to safety from the Fairlight cliffs, she thought.

"Miss Spencer, can I take one of the KS3 maths tests home?" Rosie asked as she practically skipped into the classroom.

"Absolutely, let's get one from the cupboard."

Hannah watched as they shuffled through paperwork. She wondered how she'd managed to get caught up in a date with her daughter's teacher. Dating was supposed to be off limits until Rosie was much older. And dating someone who was so far out of her league could only lead to heartbreak.

It'll be fine, she reminded herself before panic set in. *It will be a date or two, and then it will fizzle out. Once she sees how we live and she realises how time-consuming it is to be a single parent, she'll be gone.*

15

DINNER ABOVE THE POST OFFICE

ALICE LOOKED at her reflection in her full-length bedroom mirror and tilted her head to the side. The red dress was nice, but she wondered if it was *too* nice. It was Saturday night, and she was getting ready to go to the Halls' apartment for dinner. A date. She still couldn't believe she'd gained the courage to ask Hannah out on a date. The question had burst from her lips without her permission.

She also couldn't believe she was stupid enough to ask the single mother of a five-year-old out for a *drink*. Thank goodness Hannah had recovered the conversation and offered her an olive branch in the shape of a dinner at her home.

She had been surprised when Hannah had offered the compromise, and from the look on Hannah's face she'd been just as surprised as Alice had been.

She shook her head and stepped away from the mirror. The red dress *was* too nice, and it wasn't practical. She reached back and tugged the zip down. She needed an outfit that was nice but casual. Something that she'd be able to move in, something that clearly gave the message to Hannah that this was a date, but also an outfit that wouldn't scar Rosie for life.

She kicked off the dress and stood in front of her open wardrobe.

In her entire career, she'd never dated a parent of a student before. She knew teachers who had, and also knew that she'd have to advise Hardaker if things became serious. She wasn't about to jeopardise her career or Rosie's education due to any conflict of interest claims.

She considered a pair of smart black trousers. Elegant, could be dressed up or down. As she tugged them on, she remembered Hannah's expression and the casual way she spoken about the dinner invitation.

It hadn't been nerves, more a predetermined assessment that the date wouldn't progress to much more. Something in Hannah's tone and body language had screamed that she didn't believe for a second that anything would come of the date. Alice got the impression that it was a dinner invite of politeness rather than genuine interest.

After some consideration, she'd decided that Hannah's reaction had been the result of her ridiculous suggestion that they go out for a drink. Presumably that had given Hannah quite the wrong impression about her. Alice had just said the first thing that came into her mind, a drink. The classic way of suggesting that you'd like to see someone in a more relaxed setting.

Hannah had been polite but obviously distant. Her walls were firmly up.

It had hurt a little. Of course it had. She'd put her feelings out there for them both to see, and Hannah in return seemed uninterested.

Alice had two choices. One: go to dinner, smile politely, eat, and dutifully wait for the evening to end before never speaking of it again. Two: demonstrate to Hannah that she was genuinely interested and that she had something to offer the mother and daughter.

She'd gone for option two. Not that she quite knew how to pull that off, but she'd do her very best.

She pulled on a long-sleeved, plunge-neck top in crimson red and returned to the mirror to assess her appearance. She squinted and wondered what Hannah would think. Although she'd only seen the woman a couple of times, she couldn't get her out of her mind. For some reason, Hannah's opinion on her appearance mattered in a way that she wished it didn't.

Alice wished that she could be confident in herself, but her brain didn't work like that. She wasn't crippled with anxiety, but she wasn't self-assured either. That was one of the reasons she hadn't dated in a while, a niggling lack of belief that anyone would want to be with her.

A few days in quiet Fairlight had highlighted the need for her to get out of her comfort zone or face being single forever. If she hadn't managed to find anyone to date in Manchester by being a wallflower, the chances of seeing anyone in Fairlight under those circumstances were absolute zero.

Which probably explained why she had pounced on the very first lesbian she had come across. Of course, it helped that she already found Hannah Hall attractive and had wished upon a star that, by some miracle, the woman might be interested in her. When her sexuality had been announced, despite the fact that a schoolyard bully had done so, Alice knew she had to act fast or forever be tied up in knots with nerves.

She looked at her reflection one last time before reminding herself that nothing would change about how she saw herself. She hoped that Hannah would like what she saw and be willing to give her a chance.

Alice parked her car in the street next to the post office. She took a few seconds to gather some courage and then flung open her car door. She walked to the front door and pressed the intercom.

A few seconds passed and then a buzzing noise sounded. She pushed the unlocked door and entered into a dark, narrow corridor with a steep flight of stairs.

She swallowed down her nerves. She hated narrow stairs. And the dark. A light appeared at the top of the stairwell, and Rosie Hall's head appeared.

"Hello, Miss Spencer!" she greeted with excitement.

"Good evening, Rosie," she replied. She gripped the handrail and pulled herself up the stairs.

She carefully placed one foot in front of the other, reminding herself that the chance of falling was very small. Especially with all the care and attention she took to her steps. She tried to appear calm with the whole situation for Rosie's sake and was pleased when the girl stood to one side to let her into the apartment, seemingly unaware of the near panic attack state she was in.

"You drive a Mini," Rosie announced the moment she entered the apartment. She stood in a kitchenette that overlooked the street. A small dining table stood against the wall to her right.

"I do." Alice said as little as possible while she tried to get her breathing under control.

"It's cute," Rosie added. She rushed back over to a window and pressed her face to the glass to peer down at the street level.

"Can I take your coat?"

Alice was surprised by Hannah's sudden arrival behind her.

"Thank you." Alice shrugged out of the coat.

"Not used to stairs?" Hannah asked as she took the garment, clearly having noticed her short breaths.

"Not a fan of heights," Alice reminded her.

Hannah looked apologetic. "Oh, yes, well, if the stairs affect you like this, then I'm even more impressed that you managed to get up that ladder."

"I'm claustrophobic, and I don't like the dark," Alice said, she figured she might as well be honest about her many phobias up front.

"Was there a two-for-one deal on fears?" Hannah asked playfully.

"Yes, I love a bargain," Alice joked back, relieved that Hannah had taken the information in stride. She was also pleased to note that Hannah wore a casual, low-cut top and was sporting a little more makeup than she had on their previous encounters.

She subtly looked around the apartment, trying to take it all in without appearing nosey. It was small and run-down, but homely. The furniture was a little dated, but everything was clean and well presented, with nice accents in the form of cushions and custom paintwork.

"Would you like to see my room?" Rosie asked, appearing right in front of her and staring up at her eagerly. She couldn't believe this was the girl who had steadfastly refused to speak to her for two whole days of school.

"I'd love to, if that's okay with your mother?" She turned to Hannah who had hung up her coat and was now preparing food.

"I think you better, before Rosie bursts with excitement."

Permission granted, Rosie grabbed hold of Alice's hand and dragged her through the kitchen and living area and into a small corridor and then into her bedroom. There was a single wooden-framed bed which had been painted a light pink, an old-fashioned wardrobe, a tiny desk and chair, and a few shelves. Alice noted that there were not an abundance of toys or cuddly creatures, but there were books and paper and colouring pens.

"These are the books I got from the library this week." Rosie scooped them up from the shelf and started to lay them on the desk. "These I've already read, and these I'll probably read this weekend."

"I bet you've never had to worry about late fees," Alice quipped.

"No. It's twenty-five pence per day, per item," Rosie told her, all seriousness.

"So, how much would the charge be if all of these books were one day late?" Alice asked, unable to resist the temptation to test Rosie's skills.

"Two pounds," Rosie replied in a flash.

"What if half of them were four days late?" Alice asked.

Rosie paused a moment. "Four pounds."

Fractions and multiplication ticked off, Alice nodded and smiled.

"Have you always been a teacher?" Rosie asked.

"I have, since I graduated."

"Why did you come to Fairlight?"

"I wanted a change. I used to work in a big city, and I thought it would be nice to work somewhere else."

"Are you married?"

"No." Alice chuckled. She was used to the quick-fire interrogation of a child. She found it refreshing compared to the beating around the bush that most adults did.

"Do you have children?"

"A whole class of them." Alice winked.

Rosie laughed.

"Dinner's ready," Hannah called out from the kitchen.

Rosie's eyes lit up. "We're having chicken pie and mash."

"I know, it sounds delicious," Alice said, remembering Hannah's sweet text to ask about any allergies or food dislikes.

She followed Rosie from the room, noting only one other doorway in the corridor, which she presumed led to the bathroom. She wondered where Hannah's bedroom was and if she had missed another doorway at some point.

Before she had much chance to think about it, Hannah was pulling out a chair for her and gesturing for her to sit down.

Alice hesitated. "Can I help with anything?"

"It's fine, can I get you some wine? Juice? Water?"

"Could I have some water? I'm driving." Alice sat down.

Hannah quickly served plates of food and drinks, and they started to eat.

"So, did Rosie show you her books?" Hannah asked.

"She did. I think you'll need another trip to the library soon," Alice commented.

"Or the school library," Rosie said. "There's lots of books there that aren't in the library in town. Is there a maximum number of books you can take out?"

"Yes," Hannah said quickly. "One at a time. Leave some for the other students."

Rosie grumbled about the book ban.

Alice chuckled. "Probably best. You can go every day, so you'll not need more than one anyway."

"And you need to do more than just read all the time," Hannah said. "You need to go outside and breathe some fresh air."

"I walk to school and back every day," Rosie argued.

"True, but it's not enough. Do you know how many steps you're meant to do a day?"

"Over ten thousand," Rosie answered quickly.

Hannah paused. "Well, I asked for that, of course you know."

"Some people think that counting steps is silly and

that it's what kind of activity you do that matters," Rosie added.

"She's right," Alice said. "The idea of walking ten thousand steps a day was actually invented as part of a marketing campaign in the 1960s for the Tokyo Olympics."

"Are you two ganging up on me?" Hannah asked playfully.

Alice smiled. "No, I agree that Rosie should be out in the fresh air and doing exercise. I just don't think counting steps is the right way to monitor what she does."

"Reading is exercise for the brain," Rosie said.

"Your brain is exercised enough. If you keep reading, your winter hat won't fit." Hannah pointed her fork towards Rosie's head.

"That's silly," Rosie replied.

Alice watched the playful banter between them with delight. Hannah obviously had a well-tuned sense of humour and enjoyed teasing people with it.

"Your granddad won't recognise you," she continued. "He'll ask me who that big-headed, pasty-looking child is."

Rosie ignored the comment and turned back to face Alice. "My granddad is coming to visit from Scotland."

"Oh, that's nice," Alice said. "Scotland's a long way away, so I suppose you don't see him much?"

"Not very much," Rosie agreed.

"He visits when he can, but it's not as often as he'd like," Hannah added.

"He worked on oil rigs," Rosie said.

"That sounds like very interesting work," Alice said.

"What does your granddad do?" Rosie asked.

"Rosie," Hannah warned.

"It's fine," Alice reassured. "My grandfather passed away many years ago, but he was an accountant." She could see the follow-up question shining in Rosie's inquisitive eyes. "My parents are both retired, and they live in the South of France, so I don't see them very much."

Or ever, she thought bitterly.

"That's a shame," Rosie said.

Alice remained silent and ate her food. She didn't want to come out and say that she was absolutely fine with the arrangement and would far prefer the distance to having to put up with her parents' homophobic views and constant critique of her life choices.

"Rosie wants to be a doctor when she grows up," Hannah said.

"Or a vet," Rosie added.

"Maybe you could be both?" Hannah said playfully. "You could be a surgeon and put beaks on people and give frogs one big human foot?"

Rosie shook her head and looked at Alice. "I'm sorry that my mummy is so silly, Miss Spencer," she said seriously.

Alice smothered a smile and looked at Hannah. "That's quite all right, Rosie. I'm rather keen on her brand of humour."

16

BEDTIME STORIES

THE EVENING SEEMED to go by in the blink of an eye. Alice was enjoying Hannah's jokes and Rosie's inquisitive mind and was disappointed when Rosie's bedtime rolled around. The adults had been sitting on the sofa while Rosie entertained them with stories and asked Alice questions, often running around the living area with impressive bursts of energy.

"What time is it?" Hannah asked Rosie knowingly.

Rosie let out a dramatic sigh.

"That's not an answer," Hannah said as Rosie flopped over onto the coffee table.

"Bedtime," Rosie mumbled, her nose pressed against the wood.

"Actually, it's thirty minutes after bedtime," Hannah explained. "You better go and get ready for bed."

Rosie peeled herself off the table and trudged towards her room. Alice smiled at the typical behaviour. Rosie was anything but a typical child in so many ways, so when she started to act like a five-year-old it was a pleasure to see, even if it was the traditional complaint about bedtime.

"I'm a terrible mother for wanting her to go to bed at a reasonable time," Hannah explained.

"Aren't all mothers?"

"Not all," Hannah replied cryptically. She reached for her drink, and Alice decided not to follow up on the remark.

"Rosie really is wonderful, and you're wonderful with her," Alice said. "Even if you do enforce strict bedtimes."

"Thank you," Hannah said. "I try my best with her, but it's not easy."

Rosie ran back into the room and skidded to a halt in front of Hannah. She leaned forward, opened her mouth wide and breathed directly into Hannah's face.

"Mmm, minty. Now time for PJs."

Rosie nodded and then sprinted away.

Alice laughed. "I take it that's the toothbrush test?"

"Yes, don't you do that at home?" Hannah asked.

"Sadly, I live alone."

"Maybe get a pet?" Hannah suggested.

"I think the RSPCA might frown at that idea."

Rosie came rushing back into the room wearing dinosaur pyjamas.

"I offered her Disney princesses, but she wanted dinosaurs," Hannah explained before Alice said anything.

"They look amazing," Alice said to Rosie. "I wish I had some!"

Rosie fidgeted nervously and walked over to her mother, climbing up the arm of the sofa and whispering something in her ear. Hannah listened and then shrugged her shoulders.

"I don't know, pumpkin, you'll have to ask her," Hannah said.

Rosie stared at her mother and gestured her head with annoyance, indicating that she wanted her to ask Alice instead.

Hannah chuckled and turned to look at her. "Would you mind putting Rosie to bed and reading to her? Just five to ten minutes, and then snatch the book out of her hands or she'll read all night."

Alice was surprised, but she put her water glass down on the table all the same. "Oh, right, yes, I'd love to." She stood and wiped her sweaty palms on her trousers. She'd never put a child to bed before. Looking after children during the day when they were awake was easy, but this was new territory. She let Rosie lead her to her room, keen that the young girl didn't pick up on her anxiety.

Rosie turned on a small lamp on her headboard and jumped into bed. A book was laying on the bedside table. The girl pointed to it and patted the space beside her on the bed.

Alice grabbed the book and sat on the edge of the bed, bringing her legs up and stretching out.

"Mummy doesn't let me read for too long before bed," Rosie said.

"That's very wise. If she didn't, I bet you'd read all night and be tired for school in the morning," Alice said.

"That's what she says." Rosie laid down and brought the duvet up to her neck.

Alice flipped open the book and found a well-used

bookmark. She started to read, glancing at her watch to make a note of the time as she did. Rosie fidgeted as she read, tossing and turning and eventually cuddling up to her to see the book for herself.

Alice was surprised by how the rest of the world seemed to fade away. All her worries and stresses disappeared as she sat on the small bed, reading about dragons and princesses with Rosie burrowing into her side.

Ten minutes passed, and she found an appropriate place to stop reading. She put the bookmark in place and closed the book.

"Thank you for coming to dinner, Miss Spencer," Rosie whispered. Alice could feel the girl drifting off as she spoke.

"Thank you for having me." She pushed herself up off the bed and put the book back where she found it. Rosie slid down in the bed, and Alice adjusted the duvet so she was tucked in.

"Sweet dreams."

"Night, night," Rosie said.

Alice turned the light off and quietly walked out of the room, closing the door behind her.

She walked back into the living room to see Hannah on her phone.

"All go okay?" she asked, pocketing the device.

"Yes, it was fine." Alice wondered what was next. She wanted to stay, wanted to talk more, but Hannah had initially been unsure of the idea of a date at all. If this was a polite dinner, then it would now surely be over.

"Can I get you some wine?" Hannah offered. "Or some juice, as you're driving?"

"I'd love some juice," Alice replied eagerly. She had loved spending the time with Hannah and Rosie, but she was looking forward to having some time with Hannah on her own.

"Orange okay?" Hannah asked.

"Perfect."

She sat down, and Hannah went to get the drinks. Her heart started racing. This was the moment, the time where the date, if it was a real date, started. A glass of orange juice appeared in front of her, and she took it.

"Thank you."

Hannah sat beside her. "Sorry about Rosie's endless questions. She takes curiosity to new heights."

"It's fine, children are like that."

"They are, Rosie definitely is. She has no qualms asking anyone anything. When she was younger, she asked one of my clients why she was so old."

Alice laughed. "I bet that went down well."

"Luckily, she's cute and got away with it."

"You're a hairdresser, if I recall?"

"Yep." Hannah sat back, her arms stretched across the back of the sofa and crossed her legs. "Used all my educational skills wisely."

Alice licked her lips. She had detected a bit of a chip on Hannah's shoulder. Clearly she was uncomfortable with herself and her level of education. Having a gifted daughter had obviously highlighted her own educational shortcomings, and Hannah felt belittled by it.

"Hairdressing is a good profession. Creative and something that many people can't do," Alice replied. "You saw my painting skills, zero creativity."

"True, that was bad," Hannah agreed.

Alice looked around the room. Something was bothering her, and she had to ask.

"I'm sorry to be nosey, but—and please, don't take this the wrong way—but where is your bedroom? I've seen Rosie's room and the bathroom, but I can't see another door."

Hannah chuckled mirthlessly. Alice got the impression that Hannah had been waiting for this moment, as if the whole evening had been a forgone conclusion heading towards whatever was about to be said.

Hannah leaned forward and swiped up her wine glass. "You're sitting in it."

Alice looked around in confusion.

"This is a one-bedroom place. I give Rosie the bedroom, and I sleep on the sofa." Hannah knocked back a couple of gulps of wine. "This is life when you're an uneducated single mother. Feel free to run away, I wouldn't blame you."

Hannah's attitude was starting to make sense. She was embarrassed, and she expected a certain reaction from Alice. She'd been distant because she assumed that Alice would hear about her living arrangements and bolt for the door.

"Why would I run away? You've sacrificed your personal space so your daughter can have a bedroom, that's commendable. Many people wouldn't do that." Alice looked around the room. "Though I'm curious where you keep your belongings because this just looks like a living room."

Hannah gestured towards a storage unit in the corner.

"Some clothes are in there. And there's a pull-out section under this sofa for bedding."

"Ah, I see."

"It wasn't supposed to be permanent," Hannah said. "But time flies by and money flies right out the window. You don't have to be kind, I know our situation isn't for everyone. If you want to go, then don't feel obligated to stay."

"I don't want to go," Alice said. "Unless I'm not welcome. Rosie is a wonderful girl, and not just because of her gifted status, but also because she has clearly grown up surrounded by love. The fact that you sleep in here shows that you're focused on Rosie's wellbeing. That's a very admirable quality."

Hannah's bravado seemed to falter a bit. "Thank you," she whispered.

"Just being honest."

Hannah put her wine glass back down on the table and rubbed her face with her hands. "Sorry if I've been a bit standoffish. I haven't dated properly for years. A couple of dates here and there, but no one ever wanted to stay the course because of the mess my life was in. So, I kind of swore myself off of dating, until Rosie is older and I get myself sorted out."

Alice's heart soared at the realisation that Hannah must have seen something in her in order to break her self-imposed no-dating rule.

"Well, I'm glad you made an exception for me. I'd like the chance to get you know you better, if you don't mind?"

"I'd like that," Hannah confessed. She sighed. "Though I have to warn you that our life here is crazy."

"I can imagine. Being a single mum can't be easy."

"It's not. And I'd rather Rosie didn't know we were dating unless things become more serious. I've told her that you're a friend and I'd like to keep to that story."

Alice nodded. "I agree. We don't want whatever this is to affect Rosie."

Hannah regarded her for a few moments, seemingly sizing her up. "So, Miss Spencer, why Fairlight of all places?"

Alice chuckled. "I'd been working in Manchester for a few years, a big central city school which was being run into the ground by budget cuts. The kids were out of control, and everything was about targets and nothing about welfare. I kept speaking up, but I was ignored. Eventually, I decided to get out. I couldn't take seeing so many kids being swept up in a system that was just about numbers and results. I wanted to go somewhere quieter."

Hannah snorted. "You found that all right."

"Yes, it's quite different from the city." Alice turned and rested her temple against the back of the sofa. "Do you like it here?"

"In Fairlight?" Hannah asked. She shook her head. "Not much."

"Why stay?"

"Never really had the chance to leave. It's all I've ever known. I don't like it here, but I know it. It's not that bad, and it's safe for Rosie." Hannah sipped some wine. "She couldn't do anything in this village without me hearing about it."

Alice laughed. "Yes, I've got the impression that they like their gossip here."

"It's like the bricks and mortar that holds the place together," Hannah agreed. Her eyes flicked up to meet Alice's. "I bet you've heard some tales about me."

"No. I don't listen to gossip."

"No?" Hannah raised an eyebrow.

"No. I've been the subject of gossip enough in the past to know what it feels like. And most of the time it's wrong. I'd rather get the story straight from the source, if the source wants to tell it."

Hannah sipped her wine and looked thoughtful for a few moments. "How's working for Hardaker?" she eventually asked.

Alice rolled her eyes. "Well, I thought budget cuts in Manchester were bad."

"Hardaker hasn't put his hand in his pocket for decades," Hannah explained.

"I'm beginning to notice that. Of course, he didn't mention that during the interview."

Hannah laughed. "I can't imagine Hardaker interviewing anyone. How did that go?"

Alice covered her face with her hand. "It was horrible."

"Oh, there's a story. Spill," Hannah ordered.

Alice took a deep breath and then started to tell the story of the terrible interview, explaining how she got lost and turned up late and how Hardaker had called her Miss Spicer throughout the interview until she corrected him at the end. It had been thoroughly embarrassing and she'd been shocked to hear back that she got the job. Hannah joked that they were desperate, and she probably could have turned up and conducted the entire interview in a foreign language and still been successful.

They chatted comfortably for the next couple of hours, keeping to light topics and sharing anecdotes.

Alice had heard people talk about an instant attraction, but she'd never experienced one before. She'd always thought it was purely sexual. But she felt a connection to Hannah Hall like she had never known previously. Talking to her was natural and fun. She wanted to know everything but was still nervous to mess everything up. She felt more alive than she had in a long time.

Eventually, Hannah smothered a yawn behind her hand and Alice knew it was time to go, even if she desperately didn't want to. Hannah was a mother and staying up all night to chat was off the cards. She had someone else to think about. Alice needed to respect that.

"I'm sorry," Hannah said. "It's been a long day."

"It's fine, it's late." She stood up. "Thank you so much for dinner, it was wonderful."

"You're easily pleased." Hannah got up and gestured towards the front door.

"I'm useless at cooking and appreciate a home-cooked meal," Alice said.

Hannah retrieved her coat from a hook. "Then we'll have to do this again sometime."

Alice beamed. "I'd really like that." She put her coat on, and Hannah opened the door for her.

"Me, too," Hannah admitted. She leaned forward and placed a soft, chaste kiss on Alice's right cheek. Alice's breath caught in her chest.

"I'll call you," Hannah said softly.

"Great," Alice said. She waved and then stopped when

she realised how ridiculously geeky the gesture was. "Good night."

She turned and made her way down the stairs, not worrying nearly so much about them as she had when she'd arrived. Instead, she was reliving the kiss on her cheek over and over again, knowing that the second she got outside, and out of sight, she'd celebrate with a fist pump of joy.

"So, then I'll feather the back to get some of the weight out," Hannah explained to Mrs Silvestri.

The older woman met her eyes in the mirror and slowly nodded before returning to her magazine. Hannah suspected she could have cut any style she liked when it came to Mrs Silvestri. The woman seemed utterly unfazed by anything. She came in once a month, always requesting an early appointment. She politely greeted Hannah and then stuck her nose in a magazine and didn't resurface again until Hannah was finished.

Small talk was a part of the job, but Hannah had to admit she enjoyed the break that came with Mrs Silvestri. She wasn't scrambling to come up with conversation. She could simply cut hair and think about other things, like if Adrian had managed to get Rosie to school on time. And if she'd remembered to set up the new direct debit for the electricity company. And, of course, her date at the weekend.

Sunday had gone by in a bit of a daze. Hannah had

told Rosie it was simply because she was tired, but the truth was, her brain was full of Rosie's teacher.

The shop door opened, and Adrian walked in.

"Morning, ladies," he greeted.

"Morning," Hannah replied.

Mrs Silvestri nodded and then returned to her article on the top five must-have liquid foundations of the season.

Adrian walked into the middle of the shop and started to take off his coat. Hannah tried to focus on the haircut but could feel eyes burrowing into the back of her head. She looked up at the mirror and met Adrian's gaze.

She raised her eyebrow in a silent question.

He raised his own eyebrow in response and gave her a knowing look before heading into the staff room.

What was that about? she wondered. She'd have to ask once she was done with Mrs Silvestri.

"Do you want any more weight out of the back?" Hannah asked.

Her client looked up and lifted a hand to feel the back of her hair. She silently shook her head.

Hannah let out a soft sigh. The lack of gossip was nice, but a little interaction wouldn't have gone amiss.

Half an hour later, Mrs Silvestri paid and left. Hannah quickly swept the floor and prepared her workspace for the next client before heading into the staff room.

"What was that look for?" she demanded.

Adrian looked up from his phone. "I met Miss Spencer."

Hannah felt the heat on her cheeks. She tried to look nonchalant as she made herself a cup of tea. "Oh?" she asked, hiding her face in the cupboard under the guise of selecting the perfect mug.

"Firstly, she's insanely hot. Secondly, I thought she was going to tear me limb from limb," Adrian said.

"Why? What did you do?"

"Nothing. I literally just walked Rosie into the playground, and she was there, demanding to know who I was."

"Demanding?" Hannah asked with a snigger. It didn't sound anything like the woman she knew.

"Well, asking," Adrian amended. "But she was all red eyes and breathing fire about it. Very protective of Rosie. I was only saved from certain death by Rosie vouching for who I am."

Hannah couldn't help but smile at the mental image. It felt good to know that Rosie was being looked after at home, the salon, and now at school.

"I'm sure she would have done the same for any other student. It's part of the teachers' jobs, making sure the kids are with the right people," Hannah explained, still with her head in the cupboard.

"For pickups, absolutely," Adrian agreed, "but I was dropping her off. She looked very happy to see Rosie and very upset when she saw *me*. So, spill."

Hannah slowly turned around. "We might have had dinner on Saturday."

Adrian grinned. "Was it a date?"

"Ade," she chastised him and turned back to the counter to make her drink.

"Oh, come on. Was it?"

"Yes," she muttered, irritated at how she couldn't have any secrets from him. It had been less than forty-eight hours, and he already knew. "You might as well know everything. She asked, I said yes, it was dinner, Rosie thinks she's amazing, I kissed her cheek. The end."

"A kiss on the cheek?" Adrian latched onto the most pertinent fact to his mind. "Nice, classy. I like it."

"Well, I'm sure it won't last," Hannah said. "Tea?" She turned and waggled a mug in his direction.

"Yes, please. Why don't you think it will last?"

She laughed as she made him a cup. "Because it won't be long before she realises what she's getting into." The thought had cast a shadow over her memories of an enjoyable evening. She was waiting for Miss Spencer to realise that the reality of their life was too much for her to get involved in.

"You two are a catch. She'd be mad to not want to be with you," Adrian said.

Hannah put a mug in front of him. "You're delusional. Single mother, broke, not exactly in a runaway career—no offence—and I don't even have a bed to sleep in. She'll realise soon enough and will slip away."

"How about not being so defeatist and giving it a go before you convince yourself it's over?" Adrian suggested.

"That's not up to me, that's up to... her." Hannah let out a sigh.

"What?"

She chewed her lip, wondering if she should admit to the biggest issue of them all.

"What's wrong?" Adrian asked again.

"I… I don't even know her name. Just that she's Miss Spencer. Now I feel weird to ask!"

Adrian burst out laughing. Hannah glared at him before throwing a tea towel at his face.

"Oh my god, that's priceless. You've had a *date* with the woman, and you don't even know her name. Thank goodness you didn't get lucky, that would have been some weird sex talk. 'Oh… Miss Spencer… there! Right there!'"

The shop bell rang and saved Adrian's life.

Hannah gave him a playful shove as she passed by. "You're not funny," she muttered as she walked out of the staff room to deal with her next client.

18

MAKING AN APPOINTMENT

ALICE HELPED the last student with their coat and stood up.

"Right, class. Class." She waited a moment until the chattering quietened down. "Thank you," she said. "The bell is about to ring for lunch, so please walk and do not run as some of you did last week. I know sandwiches are exciting, but let's be safe."

The class giggled, and she opened the door at the very moment the bell rang. As the children filed out of the room, Alice saw Rosie approaching her. Just the student she'd been looking for.

"Rosie, may I have a quick word?" she asked.

Rosie stepped to one side. The corridor was becoming noisy with the sound of children shouting and the hammering of feet. Alice closed the door, not wanting anyone to overhear her.

"Um, Rosie," she started nervously. "Your mother is a hairdresser, isn't she?"

Rosie nodded.

"I was wondering if you could tell me where she works?" Alice felt bad about getting Rosie involved in her little scheme to see Hannah again. She knew she could have texted, but she was too nervous, and she really did need to get her hair cut. She figured she could casually call the salon and book an appointment, pretending to not know Hannah worked there.

Rosie nodded. "Yes, she works at Chopz on the high street." She let out a heavy sigh. "They spell it with a Z at the end."

"Oh dear," Alice said.

"I know. But Mummy didn't have anything to do with naming it, that was all Uncle Adrian," Rosie explained.

"Well, that's a relief." Alice winked. "Thank you, Rosie. Run along and enjoy your lunch."

She opened the door, and Rosie hurried out of the room to join the rest of the children leaving the building. She closed the door and sat at her desk. Thoughts of Hannah Hall had filled her mind ever since Saturday night, and she was desperate to see the woman again. She'd thought she'd see her in the morning when she dropped Rosie off at school, even going as far as to practise what she'd say.

All of that went out of the window when Rosie had turned up with a man. In hindsight, she may have been a little forceful in her questioning of him, but who could blame her? She was Rosie's teacher and well aware that there was no man in her life, until she suddenly turned up with one.

Of course, she'd be as cautious for any of her students, but she had to confess that she was extra watchful over Rosie who already held a special place in her heart.

She unlocked her phone and searched for Chopz on the local high street. Within a few seconds she was presented with a telephone number to make an appointment.

"It's just a haircut," she told herself. "Nothing pushy. Just… hair."

She took a deep breath and dialled the number before she lost her courage.

"Good morning, Chopz Salon. Adrian speaking, how can I help?"

She swallowed nervously. It would be just her luck to get Adrian.

"Oh, hello, it's Alice Spencer, Rosie's teacher. We met this morning."

"Ah, hello, Miss Spencer," he said, much too loudly. "How can I help?"

"I was hoping I could make an appointment?"

"Absolutely, cut and blow dry?" he asked.

"Yes, please." She wiped her palms on her trousers. "Sooner rather than later, if possible?"

"Of course." She could hear the sound of papers being shuffled. "I have something with our senior stylist this afternoon if that's suitable?"

Senior stylist? she wondered. *Was that Hannah?* She had no idea, and she was too nervous to ask. She didn't want it to be obvious that this was her way of seeing more of Hannah.

"That sounds wonderful," she said.

"Four-fifteen?" he asked.

"Perfect."

"You know where we are? On the high street, next to the trendy café. It's the only one in town!" He chuckled and she played along.

"I know the one you mean. I'll see you this afternoon."

She tossed the phone onto some papers on her desk and twisted her neck from side to side to release the nervous pressure. It had been a long time since she'd dated, even longer since she had been genuinely interested in someone. Hannah sparked something in her that she didn't understand, including a drive to make their paths casually cross in order to spend some more time in her company.

It was a childish impulse, something that should probably be left to the form room, but she couldn't help the way she felt.

A rap on the door had her jumping out of her skin. Hardaker walked in.

"And how are we today, Miss Spencer?" he asked. He walked around the room, examining her terrible paint job. She felt the pull to defend the quality of her workmanship by pointing out the terrible conditions of the walls underneath. How could she paint brickwork which was so starved for moisture that she could see it being pulled from the brush to deep within the crevices?

"Well, thank you, headmaster. And yourself?"

"Good, good." He turned to face her. "You'll be pleased to know that the electrician will be working on our power issues this afternoon."

He had a knack of making it sound like she, and she alone, would be relieved to see the building being maintained. It was as if he thought everyone else was perfectly happy with the crumbling infrastructure.

"That is good news," she played along.

"It does mean that the power will be off this afternoon," he continued. "So, I'm afraid your painting—"

"That's fine, I'm heading off early this afternoon," she said.

"Wonderful. I'd best be off." He headed for the door, presumably for his lunchtime nap, as the other teachers referred to it.

"Before you go, headmaster." She stood up. "I have a gifted child in my class, Rosie Hall."

She could tell the name registered with him by the small smirk that graced his face.

"I see," he said but didn't continue. She'd hoped that he would pick up the thread of the conversation and tell her the best way to proceed, but that looked unlikely.

"She's very advanced for her age," she tried again.

"Good, good. I'll let you use your own discretion on this one. Keep up the good work." He was out of the door before she had another chance to speak.

She flopped back into her chair. It was obvious that she was on her own with this one, too.

She had hoped that the headmaster's usual lack of enthusiasm would be pushed to one side at the possibility of a genuine genius in their midst, but Hardaker was clearly more useless than she had first thought.

If Rosie was going to have any chance of a proper education, it was down to her.

19

THE MATCHMAKER

HANNAH WAS RELIEVED to get out of the bank. She had no idea why every retired older person in Fairlight simply *had* to use the bank at lunchtime, the only time she could go. Every time she went, she was confronted by a sea of silvery heads. They all insisted on having long chats with the cashiers about absolutely nothing.

Luckily, Adrian wasn't a strict boss. In fact, he was massively unprofessional most of the time. He'd spent most of the morning teasing her about her date which she actually didn't mind, because the banter was helping the day go by a little quicker.

She was wondering whether to drop Miss Spencer a text message, maybe arrange another date. Or was it too soon?

It had been so long since she'd been interested in someone that she'd forgotten all of the rules. How soon was too soon? Was it up to her to text? Or did she wait to be sent a message? Would she come across as too keen if she went first? Uninterested if she waited?

No wonder I avoided this for so long. It's exhausting, she thought to herself.

She entered the salon only to be confronted with Adrian's enormous grin.

"What now?" she asked.

He pretended to arrange things at the reception counter. "Oh, nothing. Just, you know, I know Miss Spencer's name."

"What? How?" She advanced on him, and he took a few steps back.

"She called. She's coming in this afternoon. You're cutting her hair," he said before taking off at a run towards the staff room.

"What?! I'll murder you!" She chased him into the back room. "What's her name?"

"Not telling." He raced around, eager to put the table between them.

"Tell me," she demanded, changing direction quickly and almost catching him.

"No. I'll take it to the grave."

"Which will be in about five seconds if you don't tell me," Hannah threatened.

The bell above the shop door rang. They stopped where they were and stared at each other over the table top.

"Temporary truce?" he offered in a breathless voice.

"As long as there are customers in the salon," she told him.

He edged around the table and into the shop to greet his client. Hannah followed him and approached the reception desk to look at the appointment book. She ran her finger down the page and let out a sigh as she saw *MISS Spencer* written in Adrian's messy scrawl.

She glared at him and mouthed, 'You're dead,' as he helped Mr Smithfield with his coat. She then went into the staff room to eat her lunch and conduct a thorough online search of all Miss Spencers who had ever taught in Manchester.

Adrian was good at keeping his promises. Firstly, he had managed to round up a lot of new appointments that kept Hannah busy all afternoon. Secondly, he refused to spill the beans about Miss Spencer's name.

Hannah wanted to hurt him, but he'd offered to pick Rosie up from school so she could spend a little more time with the ever-fussy Mrs Lucas, so she'd decided to give him a temporary reprieve.

The salon had stayed quite busy, and so she hadn't had the opportunity to get him in a headlock and demand the information she so desperately needed. Lucky for him.

She had ten minutes before Miss Spencer turned up and rushed into the staff room to give Rosie a kiss and ask her how her day was.

"It was great," Rosie enthused. "Miss Spencer gave me different work to everyone else, but we didn't tell them. It was fun."

Hannah smiled. "That's great, pumpkin. Say, do you know Miss Spencer's name?"

"Miss Spencer," Rosie replied, looking at her mother as if she were insane.

"I mean her first name, or the initial. Is it written down somewhere?" Hannah fished.

Rosie shrugged. "I don't think so. I haven't looked."

Hannah couldn't blame her. She was too young to have developed the curiosity about teachers that most students had.

She had a mental image of marrying the woman and the officiant asking if Hannah Hall took Miss Spencer to be her lawfully wedded wife. She shook her head. She'd have to ask. It would be mortifying, but she had to… and soon.

"Your four-fifteen is here," Adrian said as he walked into the staff room. "She's early—must be keen."

Hannah stared daggers at Adrian as she left the room. The second she was across the threshold she plastered a wide smile on her face. "Hey, good to see you."

Miss Spencer looked up from the framed style shot she was studying on the wall. Hannah felt her mouth go dry. The woman really was gorgeous and, for reasons she couldn't understand, interested in her.

"Shall I take your coat?" Hannah offered.

"Oh, yes, thank you." Miss Spencer turned around and started to shuck her coat off. Hannah held onto the collar and gently slid it down her shoulders. It was a gesture she performed multiple times a week, but this time felt different. The salon suddenly felt ridiculously warm.

Get it together, she told herself.

"Please, take a seat." She gestured to a black, quilted salon chair and hung up Miss Spencer's coat in the closet. She used the opportunity to take a couple of calming breaths.

When she got back, she stood behind the teacher and made eye contact with her in the mirror. "So, what are we doing?" Hannah asked. "I—I mean, with your hair?"

She was relieved to see the lightest blush on Miss Spencer's cheeks as well.

"Just a trim, it's getting a little untidy."

Hannah looked at the dark brown hair that grazed the woman's shoulders. She shook herself out of her stupor, realising that she would obviously have to touch the hair if she were to wash and cut it.

She ran her fingers through the back, feeling out the previous style and the thickness of the hair. She quickly got lost in the feel and started to run her fingers across Miss Spencer's scalp, sweeping the hair from front to back to see how it fell.

"Feathering here?" She gestured to some unruly strands. "And take some of the weight out of the top?"

"Yes, exactly. Not too—"

"Not too much off the fringe. You like to tuck it behind your ears?" Hannah guessed.

"Exactly."

"Great. Let's get you shampooed." Hannah stood back and retrieved a gown from the closet. She held it up and Miss Spencer slipped her arms in. Hannah reached around and pulled the material closed in the front, tying the gown with a loose knot.

It was obvious that her attraction was out of control. Every innocent movement felt somehow more sensual.

If I get through this haircut, it will be a miracle, she decided.

She gestured for Miss Spencer to walk through to the

next room where two luxurious leather seats leant back into basins. Again, she gestured for the woman to sit down. She plucked a towel from the pile and wrapped it around her shoulders, tucking it into the collar of the gown and her blouse.

She placed a hand on her shoulder, gently encouraging her to lean backwards and put her head into the U-shape of the basin.

She turned on the water and placed her hand over the end of the shower attachment, waiting for the water to heat up. This was usually the point where she started making small talk with her client, but nothing was coming to mind. The only thing she could think of was her desperate need to know her name, and she had no plan on the best way to ask.

"How was school? Work? Well, both?" Hannah winced, thankful that Miss Spencer couldn't see her face.

"It was good. Cold, but good."

Hannah chuckled. "Hardaker still not paying for the heating to be switched on until the bitter end?"

"He claims it's on. Supposedly, there's an electrical fault which must be true as the lights won't stop flickering, but I'm not entirely convinced it's the reason for the heating being faulty."

Hannah turned the shower head towards Miss Spencer's hair and started to run water through her thick, dark locks.

"Is the temperature okay?"

"Yes, thank you."

"The heating never really started working until January when I was at Willows," Hannah explained.

"I suspected as much. The whole school is falling apart, and the headmaster doesn't seem to care, or notice. I can't decide if he's ignorant as to how bad it is or if he is fully aware and doesn't let it worry him."

Hannah applied some shampoo to her hands and massaged it into Miss Spencer's scalp. "He's been doing the job for a million years, so it could be either," she admitted. "I'm probably not the best person to judge. I never liked him, and he never liked me."

"I'm sorry, I shouldn't be complaining about work. It's not very professional of me."

"Whatever you say here will remain here. It's the hairdresser's code of honour," Hannah promised as she rinsed the shampoo out.

"Ah, is this a little like seeing a therapist?"

"You'll have to tell me. I think that if you work at Willows a few more months, you'll probably need one."

She applied the conditioner and suddenly remembered the mandatory scalp massage that she had insisted they include for every client. Her heart thudded against her ribcage.

In a split second she wondered if she should skip it. But then what if Miss Spencer spoke to someone else and realised that Chopz always gave a scalp massage? She sucked in a quick breath, plunged her spread fingers into the thick hair, and started to gently knead.

It was an act she'd performed thousands of times, but this was the very first time it had ever felt erotic. Usually she thought of it as a little extra service that they provided to emulate the big chains. This time she wanted Miss

Spencer to enjoy it and feel the pleasure that a good scalp massage could provide.

She kneaded and massaged, slowly increasing the pressure.

A moan of pleasure escaped Miss Spencer's lips. For a split second, Hannah thought the sound had come from her own lips.

She paused and leaned close to the woman's ear. "I'm sorry, but I have to ask something…"

"Yes?" Miss Spencer asked breathlessly.

"What's your name? I've been calling you Miss Spencer, and it's driving me nuts."

She laughed heartily. "Alice. My name's Alice."

"Alice!" Hannah said triumphantly. "Thank you. It's a pleasure to meet you, Alice."

"Likewise."

She finished the scalp massage quickly, knowing that it had the ability to turn into something unprofessional if she didn't. She rinsed the remaining conditioner out of Alice's hair and then squeezed out the excess water. She wrapped a towel around the hair and placed her hand on the back of her head to encourage her to sit up.

"If you'd like to follow me," she said as she led the way back into the main salon and gestured to the chair.

Alice sat down, and Hannah could see her cheeks were a little flushed. She was pleased that she wasn't the only one so affected by the close quarters they were sharing. She recalled the appointment book and was equally happy and disappointed that there were no other bookings due. She'd have the entire salon to herself. Adrian would no doubt stay in the staff room and entertain Rosie as he often did.

She pulled up a stool and released the towel, watching the wet ringlets of hair fall. She used a comb to sort out the strands.

"I was wondering if you'd like to come over to dinner again?" Hannah asked. "Unless the chicken pie was too awful?"

Alice smiled. "It was delicious. And I'd love to, but maybe I could return the favour and invite you to my place and cook for you instead?"

Hannah concentrated on combing Alice's hair. She didn't want to refuse a kind offer, but it just wasn't practical. It was the kind of offer a non-parent would come up with, not thinking about the realities of life with a child.

"That would be lovely, but Rosie goes to bed early. I'd have to get her home… it would cut the night short."

"Oh, yes, course," Alice frowned. "I'm sorry, I didn't consider that."

"It's fine, you have to think of these things when you're a parent," Hannah replied. In the back of her mind she wondered when the things you had to think about as a parent would become too much for Alice.

"And I'd hate to cut our night short," Alice added, "so if the offer is still open to come round yours, I'd love to."

Hannah stood and fetched a pair of scissors. She wondered when to arrange the meal for. She didn't want to seem desperate, so once again, she was back to the question of timing.

"I'm free on Thursday," she said. Thursday seemed safe, three days away. Not too long, not too short.

"Thursday sounds lovely," Alice said.

Hannah smiled at her in the mirror, relieved that she

seemed to be navigating the social cues despite her lack of practice.

"Is there a local cinema?" Alice asked.

"Well, there *is*, but you being from the big city would probably laugh at it," Hannah replied. She chuckled as she thought about the amateur screen which was hastily assembled at the civic centre every Wednesday.

They drifted into conversation about the local amenities, what was in town and what needed to be sought out further afield. It was relaxed and nice. Hannah was used to the small talk that came with the job, but this was more. She wanted to know more about Alice Spencer.

She took a little longer than usual to cut and blow-dry the hair, allowing herself a little extra time running her fingers through the silky strands and leaning in to catch another sniff of Alice's perfume.

Eventually she couldn't drag it out any longer, so she reluctantly finished up. Alice paid, and they arranged to meet Thursday. The goodbye was stilted, neither knowing quite what to do in the very public space. Eventually Alice opted for an adorable wave and hurried out of the salon.

As soon as the bell rang to signal her departure, Adrian appeared. "Know her name yet?"

"Yes, no thanks to you," Hannah said. She grabbed a broom and started to sweep.

"Good, good. So, what's the gossip? Are you seeing her again?"

Hannah wanted to leave him hanging and not give him a crumb of information, but she also desperately needed someone to talk about what was happening.

"She's coming to dinner again, on Thursday."

He grinned. "Brilliant!"

"No, not brilliant," she said. She thrust the broom into his hand and picked up the dustpan and brush.

"Why not?"

"Because I'm terrified," she replied. "She's... she's really great." She swept up the hairs and put them in the bin. "I want this to work, Ade."

"It will," he reassured her.

"She came from nowhere, and now I can't stop thinking about her," she confessed. "I'm waiting for her to realise what a mess I am."

He grabbed the dustpan and brush from her hands and put them on the counter. He pulled her into a hug.

"You are gorgeous, witty, perfect. Rosie is incredible. The two of you together are amazing. What's not to love? Give it a chance, okay?"

She wrapped her arms around him and nodded into his shoulder. She needed to calm down and see what happened. She shouldn't assume the worst or fall in love too soon. The problem was, she wasn't sure she had any control over any of that anymore.

20

FEELING LEFT OUT

"How LONG DO I have to stand here?" Colin asked from his position in the corner of the room.

"For as long as I say," Alice told him.

She'd decided that sending the boy to Hardaker was completely pointless. His disruptive behaviour hadn't changed, and the deterrent of being sent to the headmaster's office wasn't working.

When Colin had taken a pen and drawn on his face in order to make the other children laugh, his first question to Alice was if he should go to see Mr Hardaker.

She'd had enough and ordered him to stand in the corner. At least that way he might overhear some of the lesson being taught and learn something. He certainly wasn't learning anything being sent out of the class all of the time.

It was also time to have another probably pointless conversation with Hardaker. He had to do something about Colin's behaviour. It wasn't her job to discipline the constant disruptive force. She was already having difficulty teaching the class as well as keeping up with Rosie's own personal curriculum.

"So, I want you all to look at your worksheets in silence," she addressed the class. "Let's see how much you can remember about last week's lesson on telling the time."

They all started working on their clock faces assignment, except for Rosie who was working on Key Stage 3 maths. The children were too young to realise that Rosie was working on different worksheets, and if they did notice, they didn't question it.

The lights flickered.

"It wasn't me," Colin said from the corner.

"I wish it was," she muttered under her breath. At least then she'd be able to fix it.

"Miss?" a girl called Siobhan put her hand up.

"Yes, Siobhan?"

"Why is the school so rubbish?"

She'd asked herself that a few times. "It's not rubbish, it's just old. And they are working on the electrics and then the lights will stop flickering."

Siobhan didn't look convinced.

"Now, remember this is in silence," Alice said, hoping to fend off a mutiny from children fed up with their poor working conditions. She walked around the room, looking over shoulders to see what was being written. When she reached Rosie, she realised she was already done with her worksheet, having started it before lunch.

She pulled out the empty chair beside her and sat down. "All done?" she asked in a soft voice.

Rosie nodded.

Alice picked up the paperwork and flipped through.

She was unsurprised to see that Rosie had blasted through the questions easily. Every time she found a gap in Rosie's knowledge, she explained to her the process required to get to the correct answer. She only ever needed do it once before it was locked into Rosie's brain. It was an incredible skill for someone so young.

She knew that she needed a more permanent solution to Rosie's education. While she was happy to teach her what she could, she couldn't do so at the cost of the other students in the class. Not to mention that Rosie deserved a more dedicated curriculum. She was exceptional, and the sky was the limit in how far she could go.

The last thing she wanted was to hold Rosie back.

She also knew that would be a difficult conversation to have with Hannah who had made it very clear that Rosie was to be treated just like any other five-year-old student, despite her being absolutely nothing like the other children in the class.

"Should I do the telling the time sheet?" Rosie asked in a whisper, gesturing at the piece of paper on her desk that the other students were working on.

"Yes, please," Alice said. She stood up and stifled a smile as Rosie snatched the sheet and raced through the questions in a matter of moments.

Something needed to be done, and it wasn't going to be easy for anyone.

Alice knew she'd find Rosie sitting with a book at afternoon break. She wasn't on duty and was therefore free to go over and speak with her.

"Not playing with your friends?" she began. She knew Rosie hadn't really made friends as such.

"No. They… they do other things," Rosie said.

"Things you're not interested in?" Alice guessed.

Rosie nodded. She put her bookmark in her book and looked up at Alice, understanding there was a conversation about to be had.

"I've marked your maths paper. You've done very well."

Rosie beamed with pride. "Will you give me more homework?"

Alice shook her head. "Not tonight. Tonight, I want you to take a break. We've been putting a lot of pressure on you with these tests, and sometimes it's good to take a break."

Rosie frowned. "I don't want a break."

I want a break, Alice thought. It was exhausting coming up with a whole other lesson plan for Rosie, as well as homework, every single day.

"Then you can read, but I won't be giving you anything specific," she said. She sat down next to Rosie, checking that no one could overhear them. "Rosie, I need you to think about the fact that you may need to go up a few years, maybe even go to another school. You're very talented."

Rosie looked shell-shocked. "I don't want to."

"I realise that, but it may be what is best for you. I will eventually run out of work to give you. You will no doubt need to take exams earlier than your classmates."

Rosie shook her head. "I don't want to leave you. I want to stay in your class."

"And I'd love to have you in my class forever, but I teach five-year-olds, and I teach them the Key Stage One curriculum. That must be very boring for you. Besides, next year you would have gone up to Mr Dixon's class anyway. That's school, going up every year. You just need to be prepared that you might do it sooner that most."

Alice hated the way Rosie's complexion had gone ashen and her bottom lip quivered at the suggestion, but she knew she had to broach it with her at some point. The sooner the girl considered the idea, the less of a shock it would be when it no doubt came.

It was very common for children to struggle to leave their form tutor, especially their first ever form tutor. But Rosie, like the other children, would have to learn to live with it.

"Not today?" Rosie asked.

"Not even this week," Alice reassured her. "Not in the near future. But it's something you need to think about. You don't want to be doing boring clock faces for the next few weeks, do you?"

Rosie giggled and shook her head. "No."

"There you go then. Don't worry, I'll make sure we get you whatever you need. If you have any questions, I'll always be here for you to ask."

Rosie threw her arms around Alice's middle. "Thank you, Miss Spencer. You're the best."

Alice was shocked by the action and gently wrapped an arm around the tiny girl. She wished she could find a way to keep Rosie with her. She wasn't ready to say goodbye, even if it was obvious to her that the girl had more intelligence than half of the teaching staff at Willows, never mind the students.

Letting go of Rosie would be hard. Explaining that it was the best for everyone to Hannah would be nearly impossible.

A SECOND DATE

HANNAH TURNED around in a slow circle, checking everything from the perspective of someone just stepping into her apartment. She wanted it to look presentable and comfortable, but not like she had spent the last hour trying to achieve that look.

A damp cloth along the kitchen countertop was the height of Hannah's preparation the last time Alice had visited. This was different. Things between them had shifted, and Hannah wanted to try a little harder to impress Alice and keep her in their sphere.

Of course, she didn't want to *look* like she was trying, though.

Her shoulders slouched. Dating was ridiculous. So many rules, questions, and fears. She wondered, not for the first time, if she was just setting herself up for failure and disappointment.

Rosie had dragged a dining chair to the window and was staring outside for Alice's car. Hannah didn't know if Rosie was too young to understand that her teacher coming to dinner was a strange occurrence or if she was too smart to mention it because she enjoyed Alice's company so much.

Miss Spencer, she reminded herself. *I have to call her Miss Spencer.*

They hadn't discussed what Rosie should call Alice, but Hannah didn't want Rosie accidentally calling her teacher by her first name in class. In fact, she didn't want Rosie knowing they were dating at all. She didn't know how Rosie would process that information, and as she was struggling to process it herself, it was best that her daughter didn't know.

Hannah opened the oven and checked on the fish pie she was baking. It wasn't what she had initially planned to cook, but Rosie's unexpected declaration of Miss Spencer's favourite meal was too good an opportunity to miss. Apparently, the class were talking about lunch and, as always, had quizzed their teacher. Hannah just hoped that Alice had been honest and not mentioned something off the top of her head.

She hadn't decided if she'd casually pretend that it was a coincidence that she had happened to cook Alice's favourite meal. Or if Rosie would rat her out the second the words passed her lips.

She glanced over at her daughter, face smooshed to the glass.

She'd give up your secrets in a second if it pleased Miss Spencer, she told herself.

Rosie's connection to Alice was getting stronger every day, something which Hannah was pleased and worried about in equal measure.

She took a deep breath to try to shift the heavy concern about the future from its place on her chest. Adrian had told her not to spend too much time worrying about all the things that could go wrong. It wasn't easy, but she was trying.

The buzzer sounded.

Rosie looked confused.

"Maybe she parked somewhere else?" Hannah suggested.

Rosie rushed to the intercom, but she paused and looked to her mother for permission. She knew better than to buzz anyone up without asking.

Hannah nodded.

Rosie pressed the button for a few long seconds and then opened the front door. She hung onto the doorframe and looked down the stairs.

"Hi, Miss Spencer!" she shouted with excitement.

"Hello, Rosie."

Hannah nervously straightened a tea towel. She wondered when she had become such a clichéd bag of nerves, awaiting first sight of her date.

Alice had barely appeared in the doorway when Rosie grabbed her hand and started to drag her towards her room.

"My granddad sent me some books, you have to see them!"

Hannah stepped forward and held up her hands. "Whoa, whoa, slow down. Let's allow me to say hello to Miss Spencer and offer her a drink before you steal her away."

Rosie rolled her eyes. "Fine, I'll get them ready."

She rushed off to her room as Hannah wondered what process was required to get three books ready for viewing. It didn't matter. She was thankful for some time alone with Alice, who was wearing a dark grey dress and light grey tights. It was classy and elegant, and all Hannah wanted to do was stare at her well-toned legs.

"Hi," Alice said timidly.

"Hey," Hannah replied.

Neither of them had moved as they stood in front of each other, nervously making and breaking eye contact.

To hell with this, Hannah thought. She stepped forward and pressed a soft kiss to Alice's cheek.

"I'm glad you're here," she said honestly.

"Me too," Alice said. She turned her head, looking like she was seeking a real kiss.

"Mum!" Rosie called out.

Alice's head snapped up, and she took a small step back.

Hannah chuckled at Alice's fast reaction.

"Be patient, Rosie," Hannah called back. "Can I get you a drink? I got some non-alcoholic wine, so you can look like you're a big girl and still drive home."

Alice laughed. "Well, who could turn that down? Thank you."

"I'm sorry I've not seen you. Things have been very hectic at the salon," Hannah apologised, only realising now how much she had missed just seeing Alice. "The period between summer ending and Christmas starting is usually dead so I need to get as much extra work as I can."

"It's okay, I understand. I've seen a lot of Adrian. Why does he always smirk when he sees me?" Alice asked.

"He thinks you're hot and knows we're dating. He's planning all the ways he can tease me about it."

Alice's eyes darkened. She took a step closer and whispered in Hannah's ear, "Only Adrian thinks I'm hot?"

Hannah felt her cheeks heat up, and for the first time in a long time, she struggled to come up with a witty retort.

"Miss Spencer?"

Alice took a step back and stared wickedly at Hannah for a second before softening her expression to a warm-hearted smile. She turned to Rosie. "I'm coming, Rosie. Now, where are these wonderful new books?"

Hannah watched them leave and let out the breath she'd been holding.

"I'm in so much trouble," she mumbled to herself.

She shook herself out of her stupor and attended to dinner. Practically everything was already done. She'd decided to keep things simple and prepare as much as possible ahead of time so she could maximise her time with Alice.

She could hear Alice and Rosie talking in Rosie's room and couldn't help but smile at Alice's enthusiastic tone. She really was wonderful with Rosie. It made Hannah wonder if maybe, just maybe, she had found someone who wouldn't mind being put in second place behind her daughter. Maybe even someone who would put her behind Rosie in the priority stakes as well. That was the dream. Someone who would commit to both of them but would always put Rosie first.

She stopped what she was doing and leaned on the counter.

Get yourself together, she told herself. *It's only the second date.*

She didn't recognise herself. She'd gone from avoiding all thoughts of dating to wanting to be in a long-term and committed relationship with someone in a matter of days. Love stories like this were confined to books and movies, they weren't real life, but somehow Hannah felt like she'd been thrown into the middle of one.

Dinner was soon ready, and she called Alice and Rosie into the dining area. She served food, ignoring Alice's raised eyebrow as fish pie was served. Drinks were prepared and a little toast performed before they started to eat.

Any worries that nerves would lead to a silent meal were firmly put to one side by Rosie's never-ending commentary about her new books, her schoolwork, and her thoughts on the general education system.

Hannah didn't say a lot. Instead she watched Alice interact with her daughter. It was such a delight to watch someone she was interested in holding a conversation with Rosie. She didn't talk down to her, wasn't too light and fluffy or too stiff and serious. She understood Rosie and pitched the conversation perfectly, something that wasn't easy considering Rosie's personality.

She enjoyed watching the exchange and chipped in occasionally. She enjoyed it so much that she realized she had allowed them to remain at the dining table for longer than she had intended. Eventually, she had to speak up as it was soon to be Rosie's bedtime which also meant time for a shower.

"I'm sorry, but I'm going to have to be boring and point out the time," Hannah said.

Rosie's face fell. "Muu—uuuuum," she whined.

"It's already later than you usually go to bed, and you need to have the world's fastest shower," Hannah explained. "And I'm going to have to help you."

She didn't say anything else, knowing that Rosie was embarrassed by the flare-up of eczema on her back which required medicated lotion to be applied. Alice didn't need to know what Rosie needed help with, and Rosie would prefer to keep it private.

"Okay," Rosie agreed.

"Say goodnight to Miss Spencer and then go and turn the shower on. I'll be there in a minute," Hannah said. She picked up the plates and put them in the sink, filling the bowl with hot water to let them soak. She wouldn't get to dealing with them until the morning, but it was worth it.

Rosie hugged Alice and said she was glad she'd come over for dinner again before running towards the bathroom.

"I'm sorry, I just need to help her with a few things," Hannah said apologetically. "Make yourself comfortable on the sofa, there's more wine in the fridge. I'll be back as soon as I can."

"Don't worry, there's no hurry. I can entertain myself, take your time," Alice insisted.

Hannah hurried to the bathroom, grabbing Rosie's forgotten pyjamas from her bed on the way.

Rosie was already in the shower when she got in there.

"Mummy?" she whispered.

Hannah leaned in close to hear her over the jets of water.

"I like Miss Spencer," Rosie said.

"I know you do, pumpkin."

Rosie nodded and continued her shower, as if she just wanted to check that her mother was aware of the fact. Hannah didn't want to mention that a blind, deaf person would be fully aware of the fact that Rosie adored Alice. She hoped that enthusiasm would die down a little as Rosie got older or—god help her—got her first romantic crush.

She helped Rosie to shower, lotion, and get dressed, and then cleaned up the devastation as Rosie brushed her teeth.

"Will Miss Spencer come over for dinner again?" Rosie asked in between taking swipes along her tongue with the bristles of the toothbrush.

"I hope so. We'll see. She might be very busy," Hannah said, already knowing the excuse she would intend to use if things went awry. Busy. It was a very flexible, very blameless excuse.

"I hope she does," Rosie said.

"If she doesn't, you'll still see her at school," Hannah explained.

"She told me the other day that I might need to go to another class, or even another school." Rosie spat out the toothpaste and rinsed her toothbrush.

Well, that was news.

"Why did she say that?" Hannah asked in confusion.

"She said she might run out of work to give me. And that I'd need to take my exams early." She turned around and looked seriously at Hannah. "The others are still learning how to tell the *time*."

Hannah almost snorted a laugh at Rosie's disgust at how far behind her the class was. As if she were a human in a class full of gorillas.

"We talked about this, pumpkin. Your brain is just too big for your friends. They want to play… and eat glue… and you want to read. We're all different."

"I know. It was really boring until Miss Spencer gave me new work."

Hannah knew this was a conversation that needed to be had soon, but not right before bed.

"We'll talk about it this weekend, I promise," she said. "For now, it's time for bed."

"I don't need anyone to read to me tonight," Rosie said.

"Okay." Hannah knew that was Rosie's way of staying up later than usual to read. She made a mental note to check in on her later to ensure she wasn't propped up in bed with a book.

In Rosie's room, Hannah closed the curtains and cleaned up a little while Rosie dived into bed and got comfortable.

Hannah leaned over and gave her daughter a kiss. "No reading. Sweet dreams, love you."

"Love you, too," Rosie said.

Hannah hurried out of the room and closed the door behind her.

She paused for a moment, fluffed her hair up in the mirror in the hall, and checked her clothes were sitting correctly. She entered the sitting room and realised something was different. The stark ceiling lights had been switched off, and the cosy lamp by the sofa was on. Two fresh glasses of wine sat on the coffee table.

She looked at the kitchen and realised it had been cleaned. The counters were clear and glistening, the washing up had been done and put away.

"You didn't have to do that," she said to Alice who was sitting on the sofa reading the local newspaper.

"I wanted to," Alice said without looking up. "This local paper is ludicrous. What counts as news is ridiculous."

"Yeah, I get it for a laugh," Hannah admitted. She sat down next to Alice.

"Like this, a segment on Fairlight throughout history. Fair enough. But this picture, supposedly of the high street from 1942 is just fog. It could be a photo of anything."

Hannah had laughed when she saw the article and was glad that Alice thought it was crazy as she did. She was still surprised that everything in the kitchen had been cleaned away. She was mentally switching gears from cleaning up and offering her guest another drink, to sitting down and relaxing with said guest.

She felt eerily comfortable, which made her feel wholly uncomfortable. Being with Alice was so easy and nice. Rosie adored her, and Hannah, well, Hannah found herself careening down that path as well.

It was only the second date, and already it felt as if things were clicking into place. Hannah, always hesitant, wanted to be sure before she allowed her heart to be trampled on. She needed to know more about Alice.

"So, have you ever dated a parent before?" she blurted out, wincing even as the words left her mouth.

Alice looked at her over the top of the newspaper. "Oh, we're doing the inquisition now?" she asked playfully.

Hannah chuckled. "Not an inquisition, just inquisitive. I want to know more about you."

Alice folded up the paper and returned it to the shelf under the coffee table.

"No, I've never dated a parent before," she replied.

"But you've dated women before?" Hannah fished, sensing that Alice was open to and maybe even expecting to be quizzed.

"I have. I've only ever dated women," Alice confessed. "I've had two relatively long-term relationships, but they were nothing too serious."

"Playing the field?" Hannah asked through a cheeky grin.

"Yes, I'm a traditional player," Alice answered sarcastically. "No, just never found the right person. You know how it goes."

"I do," Hannah agreed. "Any brothers or sisters?"

"A brother. He's a dentist, married with two children. All the things my parents think I should have done by now."

Hannah wanted to ask how old Alice was, but as cheeky as she was being with her questioning, she felt that was a step too far. She imagined early to mid-thirties. Not that it mattered to Hannah, but she wondered if it mattered to Alice. Would she think Hannah was too young? Yes, it was best to keep away from the subject altogether.

The pause while she considered the matter was enough for Alice to pick up the baton and head into the conversation with her own question.

"What about Rosie's father?"

Hannah took a deep breath. It was an obvious question. One she wasn't prepared to talk about just yet.

"He's out of the picture. And I don't want to go there right now, if that's okay?"

Alice held up her hand apologetically. "Of course, I'm sorry."

"Don't be sorry, it's a natural enough question. I just don't want to do that yet."

"It's quite all right. I know I've said it before, but I have to say it again: you do a wonderful job with Rosie. I can't imagine how hard it must be just being the two of you."

Hannah couldn't help but smile. "Rosie makes it easy. She's a great kid."

"She is," Alice agreed.

"She tells me that you said something about going up a year, or going to a different school?" Hannah tried to sound calm, but she was a little concerned that Alice had had that kind of conversation with Rosie without her knowledge.

"I wanted to prepare her for the possibility. In all likelihood, she won't be with me for the entire year. You may agree to allow her to take official exams early, or it may be better for her to be taught at a higher grade. Whatever happens, I know it's hard for first-year students to adjust to change in a normal way. Most hate the idea of moving to the second year, a new teacher, new form room, et cetera. I wanted to put the idea in Rosie's head so she had at the back of her mind that it might happen. To lessen the shock. It didn't worry her too much did it? I'm sorry if it did. I was trying to help."

"It's fine," Hannah reassured her. The explanation made sense. No decisions had been made, but she needed to prepare Rosie for the possibility. "I get where you were coming from, and I know we need to talk about Rosie's education at some point." She'd really hoped that point would be further in the future, but it seemed as if they were cruising to talk about it right then.

"I spoke to Hardaker," Alice confessed. "I informed him of…" She trailed off.

Hannah frowned.

"Can she hear us?" Alice whispered.

Hannah's eyes widened. It hadn't occurred to her that Rosie could overhear the conversation they were having about her, simply because she'd never been in a situation where she'd been entertaining someone in the living room while Rosie was trying to get to sleep.

She walked over to the old stereo system she had picked up from the local charity shop. She'd always wanted one when she was a child, but it had never happened. She decided she could splurge twenty pounds on a childhood dream as an adult. She selected one of her homemade CD mixes and turned it to a volume that would interrupt any eavesdropping but not interfere with their conversation.

"There. Now we can talk about the midnight bombing raid without the spies hearing."

Alice chuckled. "As I was saying, I informed Hardaker of Rosie's gifted status."

"Okay?"

"And he couldn't care less."

Hannah snorted. "Sounds about right. He never liked me."

Alice looked scandalised. "That should make absolutely no difference."

"It does in Fairlight. He won't lift a finger to help me. Besides, what does it matter? Rosie is fine. You've given her other work, so she's not so bored. She said she's making friends. Everything is fine." Hannah was pleased that Hardaker was the bigoted, useless article she'd always known him to be. Surely it meant that Rosie wouldn't be progressed through the years?

She wanted the best for Rosie, and she couldn't see how sending a tiny child to a higher year would be good for her.

Alice didn't seem convinced but remained silent as she took a sip from her glass.

"So," she said, "you've quizzed me about exes, what about you? Rosie's father aside."

"No one serious, certainly not in the last six years," Hannah explained. "Being a single mother is a bit of a turn-off. So is being pregnant. I dated a little, but it didn't last. I decided I was better off single." Hannah took a sip of wine.

"Then I'm very grateful you've given me a chance," Alice said.

Hannah shook her head. "You're crazy."

Alice put her glass on the table and slid a little closer. "Why am I crazy? Rosie is adorable, all cheeks and big eyes. And I think we're only about six months away from seeing her hands grow out of her sleeves."

Hannah snickered.

"And, yes, she's got an incredible brain, but she's also got an incredible *heart*. She is caring, sensitive, funny. And you're okay, I suppose." Alice grinned.

Hannah laughed. "Oh, good, I rate somewhere?"

"You do." Alice suddenly turned serious. She slid closer still. Hannah's heart thudded against her rib cage. "You fascinate me, Hannah Hall."

"I do?"

"You do." Alice nodded. "I don't understand how I can miss you so much after just a couple of days apart. I hardly know you, but I can't stop thinking about you."

Hannah dampened her dry lips, certain they would shortly have company.

"I can't stop thinking about you either," she confessed.

Alice leaned forward, tilting her head to the side as their faces drew closer and closer.

A beep sounded, and they both jumped back.

"Sorry," Hannah apologised. She pulled her phone out of her pocket and cursed the text from Adrian informing her about a schedule change for the next day. She couldn't believe that their kiss, their first kiss, had been ruined. She wondered how long it would take for either of them to build up the courage to try for it again.

She put her phone on silent and dropped it onto the coffee table. She'd barely turned around when Alice took her face in her hands and pressed warm lips against hers. Alice clearly didn't want to let the opportunity go to waste, and Hannah couldn't agree more. She placed one hand on Alice's knee and used to other to cup her face, returning the soft and passionate kiss.

Her head spun. She hadn't been expecting a kiss that evening. Maybe she would have gotten her courage up to kiss Alice on the cheek again, but she had prepared for nothing like this. She'd forgotten what it felt like to be kissed. The soft give and take was hypnotic. It had only just started, and she already never wanted it to end. Any chance of taking things slowly to try to protect her feelings had evaporated.

A distant thud caused them to pull apart. Hannah turned around and looked towards the hallway and Rosie's room. She'd forgotten that Rosie had insisted on putting herself to bed, which no doubt meant that she was reading.

"Back in a second," she said to Alice.

She scurried into Rosie's room and caught her daughter reaching for the torch which had fallen out of the bed fort she had created.

"Busted," Hannah said.

"One more page?" Rosie asked, gesturing to her book.

"No more pages. Bed." Hannah swiped the torch off the floor, turned it off, and put in on the desktop. "Should never have bought a torch for a five-year-old. Bed, Rosie, right now."

Rosie didn't hear the tone often and knew it meant business. She closed the book and put it on her bedside table.

"Night, Mummy."

Hannah left the room and closed the door behind her. She rushed back to Alice, feeling guilty at leaving her alone after the kiss they shared.

Alice stood by the sofa looking nervous and wringing her hands.

"I'm sorry, I overstepped, it's too soon—"

Hannah swiftly cupped Alice's head in both her hands and kissed her, silencing any apologies. Maybe it was too soon, but she didn't care. She wanted this, Alice wanted this. Whatever happened, happened.

She gently backed Alice up until the backs of her legs collided with the sofa. She wrapped an arm around her and softly lowered her down. It had been a long time since she'd acted like an oversexed teenager, and she wasn't going to let the chance pass her by.

Alice returned the kiss in between giggles as she fell onto the sofa, Hannah straddling her.

"Not too soon," Hannah breathed.

"I'm glad," Alice said, running her hand up Hannah's back.

"Less talking," Hannah commanded. "More kissing."

"Agreed."

Hannah didn't know how long they kissed. It felt simultaneously like forever and like half a second. It was one of those glorious moments when your brain can't cope with the input, so boring things like time management get put on the back burner.

All she knew was that she'd never felt so thoroughly kissed. But things were starting to get too heated. She pulled away and pressed her forehead to Alice's, staring into her eyes. "Wow."

"I don't usually do this on a second date," Alice reassured.

"Third?" Hannah joked.

Alice chuckled. "No, it's… this isn't like me."

Hannah hesitated. "Any regrets?"

Alice shook her head. "No, none. I just didn't want you to think… I mean, I'm happy that we… I just…"

"I think I understand," Hannah said.

This behaviour wasn't like her either. Something had drawn them together with its unseen magnetic force that they were unable to ignore. Maybe it was something as quaint as fate, but whatever it was, it pulled with the power of the moon orbiting the Earth.

She sat up and glanced at the clock. "It's ten-thirty."

Alice's eyes widened. "Oh, I have to get home. I have to do some lesson prep for tomorrow."

Hannah winced, feeling sorry for her having to work so late and guilty for being the reason she'd have to.

"I'm sorry."

"Don't be." Alice stood up. "I wouldn't change things. Would you?"

There was a vulnerability in the question that belied her confident smile.

"Wouldn't change a thing," Hannah admitted. "But we should put the brakes on a little…"

"Agreed, we're not sixteen," Alice said.

They walked over to the front door, Hannah not wanting to say goodnight. The thought of it was making her feel familiar feelings of missing Alice already. It was ridiculous. She'd never felt this way about anyone before.

Is this love? she wondered. *Or am I just that starved for company?*

"I had a lovely time. Obviously." Alice blushed.

"Me, too." Hannah kissed her on the cheek, knowing she wouldn't be able to stop if they kissed properly again. "I'll call you soon."

"Please do."

She opened the door, and they said a quiet good night to each other. Hannah watched her walk down the stairwell and out onto the street. She let out a breath. She had no idea what Alice saw in her, but she was thankful for whatever it was.

A thought niggled at the back of her head that they were moving too quickly. Since Rosie was born, Hannah had prided herself on evaluating situations and not jumping in with both feet. Now she didn't recognise herself.

She'd never been in love. She wondered if this was love, this all-encompassing urge to be with someone else. Even if she hardly knew that other person.

She closed the front door and leaned against it.

"Don't overthink it," she mumbled. "Just see what happens. No doom and gloom. No dire predictions. Stop panicking."

She focused on controlling her breathing.

A smile grew on her lips. She couldn't wait to see Alice Spencer again.

22

HOW OLD ARE YOU, MISS SPENCER?

ALICE DROVE a little faster than the speed limit. It was the first time in her entire work career that she had slept through her alarm and been awoken by her second emergency one.

She'd flown around the house as she got dressed and threw her things into her bag, constantly looking at her watch and cursing under her breath.

The other teachers at Willows were extremely lax about timekeeping, but she had never been that way. She was trying to lead by example, so turning up late wasn't on the cards. Even if it meant pressing her foot down a little too heavily on the accelerator on her way into Fairlight.

Of course, she slowed to a reasonable speed as she approached the school. You never knew when a student would forget everything about traffic safety and rush out into the road.

As she cruised along, her mind drifted to the night before. She couldn't believe she'd been horizontal on Hannah Hall's sofa for half the evening, kissing the woman as if she might disappear at any moment. She'd never been like that before now either. Fairlight was having an unexpected effect on her.

Not that she'd change a second of the evening. It may not have been her plan, but she was happy with how things ended up. Deliriously happy. There was something about Hannah Hall, something she was thoroughly enjoying.

"Speak of the devil," she mumbled as she passed the Halls walking through the school gate.

She turned into the car park and found her usual spot. She grabbed her belongings from the passenger seat and got out of the car.

"That car must be as old as you are."

She looked up and smiled at Hannah and Rosie, who had walked over. Hannah was looking at her Mini with a smirk.

"I doubt it," Alice replied, although it could be. She didn't want to have the inevitable conversation about age in the car park when she was already running late.

"Mummy is twenty-five," Rosie spoke up. "How old are you, Miss Spencer?"

"Rosie, you can't ask a lady things like that," Hannah quickly told her daughter, a red glow starting on her cheeks.

"Why not?" Rosie looked up at her mum, understanding that she had done something wrong but not understanding why.

"I'm thirty-six," Alice said, to save Rosie's blushes. She was still reeling that Hannah was only twenty-five. She'd guessed a couple of years older, hoping for at least a single-figure age gap between them.

"You're eleven years older than Mummy," Rosie helpfully added.

"Yes." Alice locked the car door.

"More than twice my age," Rosie continued.

"Y—yes." Alice wanted a hole to form in the car park and wash her out to sea that she could hear crashing against the rocks behind her.

"Good thing I like older women," Hannah said.

Alice's eyes snapped up. Hannah was staring intently at her, conveying a message that went over Rosie's head in more ways than one.

"Rosie, I can hear Simone. Why don't you go and say hello?" Hannah suggested.

"Okay." Rosie turned and ran towards the playground.

"Sorry, she's not very good with social niceties," Hannah explained.

"It's okay. It's probably good that it's out there," Alice said. She adjusted her bag and the paperwork in her arms.

"I had a great time last night," Hannah said, a smirk on her face.

Alice snorted a laugh. "So did I. Although I'm usually a bit better behaved."

"Shame." Hannah winked. "I was planning a repeat performance. Soon."

Alice felt her mouth go dry. She'd hoped that Hannah felt the same way she did, but this confirmation caused goosebumps to crawl down her arm.

The bell sounded.

"You're late, Miss Spencer," Hannah said. "I'll let you get to work. I'll call you later."

Hannah turned on her heel and went to say goodbye to Rosie. Alice shook her head to try to get herself together. She was relieved that the age issue had been aired and was, apparently, not one.

She released a deep breath and walked towards the building.

23

TO TEXT, OR NOT TO TEXT?

HANNAH FILLED the kettle and switched it on. Then she turned it off again. She didn't need another hot drink. She just wanted something to do. But if she had another hot drink, her eyes would start swimming.

She looked over at Rosie who was happily reading a book on mathematics that Alice had loaned her. It was Saturday afternoon, and the weather was terrible, rain and wind howling past the window.

Despite the conditions, she had dragged Rosie grocery shopping that morning and then to run some other errands around town. They were things that technically could have waited until Monday, but Hannah was eager to get out of the house in the hope that she would accidentally bump into a certain first-year teacher.

Sadly, Alice Spencer had been nowhere in sight.

The last couple of days had passed in a blur, and Hannah hadn't had the chance to call Alice. She meant to text her, but everything she came up with sounded too needy. Her heart was begging to see Alice again, but her brain was reminding her that they'd only had two dates. She didn't want to smother Alice before they really had a chance to get to know each other.

The pressure was on, though, because Hannah was invested. This wasn't like other casual dates she'd been on or like previous relationships where she'd always had one foot out, just in case. Alice had quickly blasted by her defences and was now nestled in her heart, with the power to break it in two.

Hannah grabbed her phone and opened a blank message to Alice. She thought for a few seconds about what to write. Casual comments, quips, and sarcasm were all pushed out the way, and she finally typed, **Thinking of you x.**

She hit the send button before she had too much time to think about it. She'd done what she said she would. She'd reached out and contacted Alice. Now the ball was in her court.

"What are you doing, pumpkin?" She walked over to Rosie, hoping to distract herself from thoughts of Alice for a while.

"Reading." Rosie didn't look up.

"Want to do something with me?"

Rosie frowned. "Like what?"

"I don't know. Something fun."

Rosie looked up and thought about it for a few seconds. "Not now, maybe later?"

Hannah stared at her daughter. Sometimes she really wondered if there had been a mix-up at the hospital. Rosie would much rather read about math than do something fun with her own mother.

"Riiiiight." Hannah turned around and looked at the apartment.

She had been meaning to clear out the cabinets for a few months. Or she could wipe down the tops of them. She looked at her phone.

No reply. She's probably freaking out because you're so clingy. Should I text again? No! No, that's clingier. Leave it.

"I'm going to watch a movie," Hannah said. "Want to watch a movie?"

Rosie shook her head.

"Okay, I'm going to watch a movie on my own then. I might make myself some popcorn." She looked at Rosie, hoping for a reaction, but nothing was forthcoming. She realised that she really would be watching a movie on her own, and she decided that she definitely would be having popcorn in the hopes that she would be able to eat away her anxiety.

Hannah had glanced at her phone every ten minutes throughout the movie. There was no reply from Alice, and her anxiety was working overtime. She couldn't ignore it anymore. She knew she had to say something else.

She unlocked the phone and opened a new message. She stared at the screen as her mind came up blank. Usually, she'd make a joke, stick to defensive humour that she liked to hide behind. But her often sharp mind couldn't come up with anything.

I'm sorry if that was too much.

She hastily typed and sent the message. The second she

sent the message, she wished she hadn't. She wished she hadn't sent any messages. Or even owned a phone.

"Mummy, I'm ready to watch a movie now." Rosie stood in front of her.

"I just finished watching a movie, pumpkin."

"You can watch another."

"I can't. I'll get square eyes."

"That's not true," Rosie said. "Your eyes don't change shape."

"Well, mine might. How about a board game?"

Rosie thought about the offer for a moment. "Scrabble?"

"Sure."

"No made-up words this time," Rosie instructed seriously.

"We'll see."

Hannah cast a final glance at her phone before getting up to fetch the Scrabble set from the shelf.

Only half her brain was focused on the game. The other half was busy constructing doomsday scenarios for her fledging relationship and cursing herself for having fallen for Alice so quickly.

It was fifty-eight excruciatingly long minutes before her phone beeped. She nearly sent it flying across the kitchen in her rush to pick it up and read the message.

Hi! Not too much at all, I've been thinking of you too x I'm sorry for the delay, been away from my phone.

As she read the message, another arrived. It was a photograph of a freshly painted classroom wall. Hannah smiled so hard her cheeks hurt. Everything was fine. They were fine. Alice had just been busy.

You missed a bit, she sent back.

"Who is it, Mummy?" Rosie asked.

"Adrian," she lied.

She stared at the three dots blinking on her screen, indicating a reply was on the way. She looked at the picture of the painted wall, hating that Alice was spending her weekend decorating the classroom. She cursed Hardaker and his rusty purse strings.

It's all well criticising when you're not here! It looks better in person, I assure you. Sadly, I have to get back to work. Missing you very much x

Hannah closed the message and opened up a new message to Adrian, asking him if he would mind taking Rosie for the afternoon and maybe into the evening. Following an afternoon of panic, she had a desire to be closer to Alice. And, she reasoned, the sooner the painting was done, the sooner Alice would have some free time. Hopefully to spend with her.

Adrian replied quickly saying he was free and would love to see his *favourite* member of the Hall family. She'd thump him for that.

"Pumpkin, Adrian wants to know if you want to go over there and spend the afternoon with him?"

...ie's face lit up. Despite seeing Adrian on a regular ...d spending all the time she could

...ady up from her seat and putting ...the bag.

...t you changed and ready to go."

It was still raining as Hannah entered the deserted school playground, but she didn't care. She'd gotten changed into her old decorating clothes and hurried Rosie to Adrian's before making her way to Willows.

She hopped up the steps and pressed on the door, only to be stopped in her tracks as the door refused to budge. She belatedly realised that Alice had, sensibly, locked the door behind her.

Grinning, she held up her phone and took a selfie of herself outside of the school door.

Let me in! I'm ready to criticise your paintwork in person!

She waited, hoping that the sound was turned on on Alice's phone. The rain continued to fall, but it didn't dampen her mood as she thought about finally seeing Miss Spencer again. It had been a just over a day, but it felt like forever.

She saw movement through the glass as Alice hurried down the stairs with a large set of keys in her hand. A few moments later, the door was unlocked and thrown open.

"You should have told me you were coming, I would have unlocked the door. You're soaked!" Alice grabbed her arm and brought her into the building.

Hannah shivered at the cold air in the school.

"Brr. It's okay, I think it was warmer out there."

Alice laughed. "True, but the one thing this buildi has going for it is that it's dry. So far." She closed locked the door again. "I'm very happy to see yo have to ask, what are you doing here?"

"Helping." Hannah gestured to her clothes. "I can paint."

Alice stared at her in surprise. "You'd seriously give up your Saturday with Rosie to come here and help me paint?"

Hannah tried to appear casual but knew her reddening cheeks would give her away. "Of course. I want to help. And see you again."

Alice surged forward and then stopped herself. "Sorry, I'm covered in wet paint."

Hannah pulled her into an embrace. "Old clothes," she explained before kissing her.

Soft, warm lips immediately melted on her own, and she felt whole again. Part of her hated that she now seemed to need Alice to feel complete, but the bigger part of her was just happy to see and feel her again.

Reluctantly she pulled back. "So, I'm here to help. Boss me about and tell me what you need. I'll even go up the death ladder."

"My hero." Alice gestured towards the stairs, and they both walked up to the top floor. "I thought that confronting your fears was supposed to help beat them into submission, but I've been up and down that ladder all day and I'm still terrified of heights."

"Maybe you need to do a bungee jump? The ladder isn't a big enough challenge for you?" Hannah joked.

Alice visibly shuddered. "No, thank you. A long time ago I decided to accept the fact that I have a great number of fears and to just do my best to avoid them."

"So, no bungee jumping with a snake wrapped around your neck? At night?" Hannah quipped.

"Stop." Alice chuckled as they walked into the form room.

"That's all of them, isn't it? Oh, and spiders. You'd need to have a spider with you!"

"And the plane would have to be on fire," Alice added, "but I think I'm safe from that particular scenario. Except for in my nightmares, so thank you for that."

"If you need to call someone in the middle of the night, you have my number," Hannah offered, grinning.

"I may hold you to that. Especially as you'd be the cause." Alice pointed to the wall. "What do you think?"

Hannah tore her eyes from Alice and looked at the freshly painted area. "Looks good." She stepped closer and really examined the work. Alice had clearly taken a lot of time and effort, even at the top of the ladder where she was terrified. It made her realise just how much Alice cared about the kids and the school.

"I can't believe you're doing all this," Hannah said.

Alice shrugged. "No one else will. To be honest, this building needs a much larger overhaul, but Hardaker will never pay for that. This is like bringing a sticking plaster to a car crash. The kids deserve a better environment to learn in. The excuse of 'it's an old building' just isn't enough."

Hannah reached into a paint bucket and picked up a brush. "Point me in the right direction."

Alice smiled. "I'm doing a second coat on this section. The brickwork soaks up paint, so it needs a lot of coats. Wish I had known that before I bought the paint."

"I can't believe you're paying for this as well as doing the work." Hannah started applying paint where Alice had shown her.

"No one else will." Alice picked up another brush and started painting a little way from where Hannah was. "But thank you for helping, I really appreciate it."

"You're welcome." Hannah painted in silence for a few moments while she thought. "Maybe if I'd had a teacher who cared as much as you do, I'd not have hated school so much."

"Was it bad?" Alice asked.

"Awful. Not just the teacher's fault. They didn't help, but it was a lot of things," Hannah admitted. "Kids can be cruel."

"They really can," Alice agreed.

The lights flickered on and off for a few moments.

"Nice disco effect you have going here," Hannah joked.

"Yes, it's really helpful in the dark weather when painting," Alice sighed. "It's been happening for a while, but it got worse after the electrician came in to supposedly fix the issue."

"Sounds about right," Hannah said.

The lights returned to normal, and she continued working.

"Where's Rosie?" Alice asked.

Hannah turned to Alice, her jaw dropping. "Rosie?!" she cried, looking deadly serious for a moment before laughing at Alice's shocked expression. "She's with Adrian."

"You're not funny," Alice said.

"I am, though."

"Okay, you are a little."

Hannah put the paintbrush down as she realised a

table covered by a dust sheet was soon going to be in her way. She pulled the table out of the way, and the sheet fell to the floor, exposing stacks of papers and books.

She crouched down and picked up the sheet, but before she covered the desk, she noticed a leaflet for an expensive-looking academy farther along the coast. She picked up the leaflet and held it up.

"Planning your escape from here already?" she asked.

Alice was focused on painting and didn't look up. "Hmm?"

"Prince Academy? Are you hunting for a new job already?"

Alice turned and looked at Hannah. "Oh, that. No, I'm locked in for the year at least. Actually, I got the details for Rosie."

Hannah felt a cold shiver run through her body.

"Rosie?" she checked.

"Yes. It's a wonderful school."

Hannah turned the leaflet over. "It's a long way away. What do you expect? A five-year-old to get the bus on her own there and back every day? It would take two hours to get there! You expect Rosie to have an eleven-hour school day? I know she enjoys school, but that's ridiculous."

Her anger was rising the more she stared at the leaflet. Who did Alice think she was? Did she really think Hannah would want to send her daughter to this school? That Hannah could even *afford* to?

Alice's mouth dropped open. "Of course not." She put her own paintbrush down. "Do you honestly think I'd consider that?"

Hannah read the leaflet properly. She was fuming.

Alice had no right to make plans for Rosie's education without consulting her. Especially these kinds of plans.

"This is something for a *parent* to decide, Alice. Not a teacher. We may be dating, but that doesn't give you any say over Rosie. Do you understand? I know you're finding it a challenge to teach Rosie and the rest of the class, but that doesn't mean you can just ship her off when the going gets tough."

A line caught her eye, and her jaw dropped open.

"This is a *boarding* school? A fucking boarding school. You seriously expect me to send my daughter here?"

"No, of course I don't," Alice replied. Her cheeks were red, her hands on her hips. "But what is so wrong with a boarding school? I went to a boarding school."

"I bet you did," Hannah said. She should have known better than to get involved with someone like Alice. She clearly came from a middle-class background and would never be able to properly understand Hannah's life and values.

"What's that supposed to mean?" Alice asked frostily.

"You have no idea, do you? You do realise that places like this cost money, right? Money that I don't have. Money that I could never even *hope* to have."

Alice held up her hand. "Stop. Stop right there. Do you really think I would suggest sending Rosie to boarding school? Do you not know me at all?"

"The evidence is right here, Alice. You even admitted you got this leaflet for Rosie. Don't try backing out of it now."

"I'm not!"

"I… I can't be here anymore." Hannah threw the leaflet back down on the table and walked out of the door.

She marched down the corridor towards the exit as she had done so many times in the past when storming out of school. She couldn't believe she had been foolish enough to think Alice would understand her or her life. She'd been stupid to give her heart to the woman. She'd known it would end in heartache, and here she was, destroyed and wondering how to tell Rosie that Miss Spencer would never, ever come to dinner again.

She pulled the door and felt the lock hold it firmly in place.

"Fuck," she mumbled.

She heard the sound of Alice rushing down the stairs.

"Hannah, wait," Alice called out.

"Unlock the door and let me out," Hannah demanded.

"Let me—"

"I don't want to hear it." Hannah pointed at the door.

Alice unlocked the door, understanding that Hannah wasn't in the mood to be messed about.

"And I don't want to see you again. Obviously, we'll remain professional for Rosie's sake, but nothing more. This was all a huge mistake."

The second the door was unlocked, Hannah marched out into the rain. Tears fell down her cheeks. She refused to turn around. This time she really would be walking out of school for the last time.

24

OVER

Adrian opened the door, took one look at Hannah, and said, "Oh god, what happened?"

"It's over," Hannah said through gritted teeth as she walked into Adrian's hallway.

He closed the door to the living room, where she assumed Rosie was. "What happened?" he asked again.

Hannah paced the hallway, still incensed by what had happened. "She wants to ship Rosie off to some snooty boarding school. She's five. FIVE. What kind of insane person wants to put a kid of that age into a boarding school? Now, I'm not saying that it wouldn't be a good thing for Rosie to get that kind of education. I'm not a moron. I know that school would give her a great start in life. But she's practically a baby. I'm not sending her to a place that looks like it's fucking haunted. And how dare she make decisions for my child without consulting me? What kind of person does that? Well?"

Adrian blinked. "You want me to talk now? Or do you

have another ten minutes of ranting to get out of your system?"

She let out a sigh and sagged against the wall. "I'm sorry. I'm just so angry. I trusted her. I… I fell for her."

"Explain what happened, exactly."

"While we were painting, I saw a leaflet for some posh academy on her desk. Miles away from here. I thought she was looking for a new job or something, but she said it was for Rosie. Then I realised it was a boarding school. We argued, and I left. I told her I never wanted to see her again."

Adrian pulled her into a hug as she started to cry again.

"I really liked her, Ade," she whispered into his shoulder.

"I don't blame you, she seemed so nice." He held her tightly. "At least you know now. At least you learned before things got really serious. I know it doesn't help right now, but it could have been so much worse."

She didn't want to admit how deeply or how quickly she had fallen for Alice, so she just nodded into his shoulder. "You're right. I don't know what I'm going to tell Rosie."

"Like you just said, she's five. You don't need to tell her anything yet. She'll ask at some point, and then you can make some excuse. But you don't have to deal with all that now. You need to look after yourself. I'm so sorry, Han. I know you've been really reticent about dating, and it's shitty that this has happened. Don't let it put you off. You'll find someone."

She didn't want to find someone. She wanted Alice to

be what she expected and not the heartless monster she had turned into. Walking through the rain towards Adrian's house, Hannah had wondered if a perfect partner for her even existed. Maybe she was hoping for someone who could never be real. Maybe her standards were too high.

It was a heart-breaking thought.

She'd managed to convince herself over the last few years that she didn't need anyone, that she was fine alone and would focus on looking for a partner when Rosie was an adult.

But Alice had made her see the light. She'd been scared and avoiding the chance of finding love because she didn't want to get hurt. Now she not only had a broken heart, but she also could no longer lie to herself that she was happy alone.

"Who is it, Uncle Adrian?" Rosie called out.

"I'll go and talk to her," Adrian said. "You pop into the kitchen and make us both a cup of tea. I'll tell her you'll be in soon, okay?"

Hannah nodded. Adrian quickly walked into the living room, closing the door behind him. Hannah looked up and saw her reflection in the mirror. She looked an absolute mess, with soaked hair and clothes, smudged mascara, and skin so white she looked like a ghost.

"Pull yourself together," she told her reflection. "It's just you and Rosie now. That's all you need."

2 5

COLIN'S BIG MISTAKE

ALICE WAS NOT surprised to see Adrian dropping Rosie off at school on Monday morning. She suspected it would be a while before she laid eyes on Hannah again. Adrian looked at her and quickly looked away, obviously aware of the situation and not wanting to be thrown into the middle of it.

She couldn't blame him.

Sunday had been her darkest day in a long time. She wanted nothing more than to stay in bed and cry over the loss of whatever it was she had had with Hannah. But she couldn't. The decorating hadn't been finished, and the classroom was still a mess. So, she had spent all day Sunday decorating while crying and shouting in frustration at herself. She couldn't believe that she had let a simple conversation get so out of hand.

If only she had not been so shell-shocked by Hannah's anger, she would have been able to respond and cool the situation down. Maybe even fix things. But she hadn't.

She'd been caught up in her own anger at Hannah's interpretation of her actions.

It had floored her that Hannah had read the leaflet and immediately hurled accusations at her. She'd responded defensively rather than calmly. She wished she could wind back time and try again.

She looked at her watch. The bell was about to ring in a few moments.

"Class One, over here, please," she called out to the playground as she planted herself to the side of the main entrance. She wanted to lead them up to the newly decorated form room herself to try to build some excitement about it.

"Why are we standing here?" Simone asked as she joined the queue.

"Because I have something to show you."

"Is it a hamster? My cousin's class got a hamster," Simone said.

"It's not a hamster."

"A tarantula?" Colin asked as he joined the line.

"Yes," Alice told him, "and it will eat anyone who hasn't done their homework."

Colin eyed her for a few long seconds. "You're lying."

"I'm joking, there's a difference."

"Is there?" he asked.

"There is. If you pay attention in English, you'll find out what it is," she told him.

The bell sounded, and the other students rushed into the building. Alice waited a few minutes until they had all cleared out of the corridors and gone into their respective form rooms. She didn't want to lead a line of slow-moving five-year-olds up a flight of stairs when the rest of the school was rushing around.

"Okay, let's go." Alice led them into the building once it was clear.

As was becoming more frequent, the lights started to flicker.

"It's not that the lights have been fixed," Colin quipped.

"I'm not a miracle worker, Colin," Alice replied.

She lined them up in the corridor outside of the classroom. "Now, I have something to show you. But this is only part one of the project, and I'll need your help for part two. Is everyone going to help?"

The children started nodding, some bouncing with excitement for whatever was about to happen. She opened the door, and they walked in.

"It's new!" Daniel shouted, never the brightest spark.

"It's newly decorated," Alice corrected.

"It's so bright!" Simone smiled. "I like it!"

Alice watched as the children strolled around the room, pointing out the new colour and commenting on how much better it looked. Suddenly all of her hard work and conquering the terrifyingly high ceilings seemed worthwhile.

Her eyes settled on Rosie, who was looking at her sadly.

So, she knows, Alice surmised. *Hannah's told her something at least.*

She tore her gaze from Rosie.

"Class, class," she said and waited for them to quieten down. "As you can see, the room has been decorated and is nice and clean and bright now. But this is only part one. As I said outside, I need your help. We need to create lots and lots of art to put on the walls to make it even better. What do you think?"

The class whooped with delight, and Alice knew she'd get a complaint from her neighbouring teachers. She didn't care. Nothing soothed the soul like a crowd of happy children.

"What are we going to make?" Colin asked.

"All kinds of things. When we learn something new and fun, we'll do some painting or make some collages, and then we'll put them on the wall."

"All of them?" Colin asked.

"Yes, unless someone really wants to take something home," Alice explained.

"Cool." Colin looked around the room with a nod.

Alice couldn't tell if he was genuinely interested in the idea or if he had an evil plan up his sleeve. With Colin it could be either.

She looked at Rosie again and noticed she was being very quiet. More so than usual.

She felt responsible. If she had not gotten involved with Hannah, it would have meant a lot less heartache all round. Especially for Rosie, who was having a hard enough time as it was without the extra emotional turbulence. What was worse, there was nothing she could do or say to fix it. It absolutely wasn't her place to bring it up with Rosie.

It was going to be the longest Monday in history.

For some of her students, the morning's enthusiasm for the newly decorated classroom had quickly turned into overexcitement. Unfortunately, it was the worst day for Alice to have to deal with the children trying to push the limits. The physical and emotional exhaustion from the weekend was catching up with her, and she was tired and sensitive.

She sat at the desk in the library and watched despondently as members of her class ran around like lunatics. They were already five minutes over the time she had allotted in the library.

"Simone, stop running around and find a book to borrow or I will choose one for you," Alice shouted.

Simone stopped immediately, rushed over to a shelf, and started to look at books.

"Miss, I feel sick," Colin said for the third time since they'd been in the library. "There's a funny smell."

"So you keep saying. Pick a book and we can go back to the form room."

Colin loved disrupting lessons, and Alice hadn't detected any funny smell, aside from the old books.

"It really stinks," Colin pressed.

"No one else can smell it. Hurry up and get a book, and then you'll be away from the supposed smell," Alice said.

He sighed and dragged himself away, complaining about the stench as he did. She really didn't have the strength to deal with Colin's behaviour today. Simone playfully tapped Daniel on the shoulder, pronounced he was it, and then ran away. Alice sighed. It was going to be one of those days.

"Five more minutes, then we have to get going, we're already late," Alice called out.

The children hurried around, obviously detecting that their usually relaxed teacher was getting stressed. Simone placed a book on the desk, and Alice helped her to sign it out of the log.

She noticed Colin and Rosie talking in the distance. Considering their history, she kept a close eye on them. They seemed to be just talking, but she didn't trust Colin as far as she could throw him.

"Miss Spencer?"

She blinked and looked at Simone who was asking her a question.

"Sorry, Simone, what did you say?"

Simone started to tell a story about what she had done at the weekend. Alice did her best to look interested and nod in the right places, but her eyes kept drifting over to the odd couple having a conversation.

Something didn't seem right.

It was break time, and Alice was on playground duty, yet again. She'd noticed that she seemed to have a higher number of duty sessions than some of her colleagues, something she was going to let slide. But now that her mood had turned foul, she was willing to bring it up with Hardaker at the next opportunity.

Fairlight, and Willows, were fast losing their appeal to her.

Lucy Gibson walked over to Alice and held out a hot

drink. "Coffee, strong, you look like you could use it," she said.

Alice took the mug. "Thank you."

"What's up? No offence, but you look terrible."

Alice wasn't about to talk about what was really wrong and allow the gossip mill of Fairlight to churn Hannah over.

"Lack of sleep," she explained. "And I've come to the end of my tether with Colin. He's been pushing me all morning. Complaining about some phantom smell."

Lucy's head snapped up. "I had a student complaining about a smell, too, but I couldn't smell anything."

"No one else could. We were in the library, which isn't the freshest of places with no windows," Alice said. She wondered if there was a smell, and Colin was the unfortunate person with a nose attuned enough to pick up on it. "Strange coincidence, though."

"Maybe our two troublemakers happened to come up with the same excuse to get away from work?" Lucy suggested.

Alice opened her mouth to reply when a loud siren started blaring from the building.

"Is that the fire alarm?" Alice shouted above the sound.

"Yes. We're not due a drill, are we?" Lucy asked.

Alice shook her head. "Not at break time." She placed her coffee mug on the wall, marched into the middle of the playground, and started shouting instructions to the students. They'd all performed a school-wide fire drill at the start of the term, and so everything was hopefully still fresh in the children's minds.

Students started lining up in their designated locations. Alice saw the rest of the teaching staff and the administrators pour out of the building. The headmaster's secretary, Cynthia, had the school registers and started handing them out to the teachers.

Alice started her roll call while keeping an ear out for what was being said by the other teachers. There was confusion, but it seemed that the fire brigade had been called.

"Daniel?" she called again, her head snapping up as she checked the line. She could immediately tell that a number of her class weren't in the line. She skipped Daniel's name and continued on. Four students were missing: Daniel, Colin, Abdul, and Rosie. Her heart slammed against her rib cage.

"What's wrong?" Lucy was beside her in an instant.

"I'm missing four." Alice started looking in the other lines and saw Daniel, and then Abdul. "Make that two."

She called out for Daniel and Abdul to stand in the correct line and then continued her search for Rosie and Colin. She walked in between the rows of students, looking for them.

"Fire from the basement," she heard one of the administrators say.

"It was already through the door by the time the alarm sounded," Hardaker was explaining to someone on the phone.

It's a real fire, she told herself. *Thank goodness it happened at break time.*

"Has anyone seen Colin Whittaker or Rosie Hall?" she shouted loudly.

Students and teachers shook their heads.

She shouted again.

Suddenly, there was a sound from the assembled crowd, a murmur of shock and fear. She turned towards the school and could see flames lapping out of one of the classrooms on the ground floor. Smoke was already billowing out of the main entrance.

Panic rose within her. Fire was one of her biggest fears. It was uncontrollable, unpredictable, and deadly.

"Miss Spencer," one of the older students said. "Is that Colin?"

She turned around and followed the girl's gaze. Sure enough, Colin was hiding inside one of the tunnels in the playground.

Alice took off at a sprint, hoping that Rosie was with him.

"Colin?" She said as she crouched down and looked into the tunnel. He was alone. "Where's Rosie?"

Tears were streaming down his face. "I dunno."

Something was wrong. Terribly wrong.

"Colin, you're not in trouble. I just need to make sure that everyone is safe. Do you know where Rosie is?"

Colin shook his head quickly. Too quickly.

"Colin, I really need your help. Please," she begged.

"It's not my fault!"

"I know, sweetheart, I know. Just… tell me. Let me fix it."

He took a deep breath. "We… we went into the library. She said she'd seen the next book in the series I'm reading, but I didn't see it. She said she could prove it to me…" He trailed off, terrified eyes staring at the burning building.

"What happened?"

"I… didn't know there would be a fire," he whispered.

"What happened?" Alice repeated firmly.

"I locked her in the store cupboard in the library. I was going to let her out after break."

Alice didn't stop to think. She turned and ran towards the building.

26

TIME TO PANIC

"When you write an appointment in the book, could you use your big boy handwriting so I can read it?" Hannah asked, squinting at Adrian's scrawl.

"Oh, come on, what are you complaining about?" He looked over her shoulder. "Agnes Banks. Is that so hard?"

"That's an A?" Hannah exclaimed.

Any further debate was silenced by the sight of a fire engine speeding past the shop with blue lights flashing and siren wailing.

"Wow," Adrian said. "Wonder what that's about."

Hannah frowned. "They're in a hurry."

Adrian was already out of the door. "I'll see what I can find out."

"You're such an old gossip!" Hannah shouted after him.

She returned her attention to the appointment book. She needed some distraction between clients. Her brain kept returning to her argument with Alice.

"Stop it," she told herself. "Just focus on work."

Adrian nearly took the door off the hinges when he threw himself back into the shop. "It's the school," he breathed.

Just as he uttered the words, Hannah's next client turned up. Adrian looked from Hannah to Mrs Allardyce.

"Hi, Mrs Allardyce, Hannah has to pop out, so I'll be dealing with you." He gestured for Hannah to make her escape.

"Thank you," she said to him. "I'll be back as soon as I can."

Within seconds, she was in the street and running like she had never run before. Other villagers were standing around, chatting and pointing. Hannah looked up. She could see plumes of thick, grey smoke over the tops of the houses.

She charged around the corner and onto the main road down towards the school. Other parents were making their way towards the school, some driving and others running like she was.

"Please, please, please, please, please," she panted as she ran.

She couldn't cope if anything happened to Rosie.

Without permission, an image of Alice floated into her mind. The thought of Alice being hurt was just as fear-inducing.

As she got closer, she could see the fire engine parked up in the playground and the officers getting equipment ready and talking with Hardaker.

She sprinted into the playground. Her eyes quickly found the first-year class, but there were two notable absences. Lucy Gibson walked towards her, eyes wide and terror-filled.

Hannah's heart sank. Something was terribly wrong.

"Where is she?" she screamed at Lucy. "Where's my daughter?"

In that second, she knew with absolute certainty that Rosie was in the building.

"Miss Spencer went in to get her," Lucy explained.

Hannah's mouth dropped open. It felt like her heart had turned to ice in her chest. Her daughter was somehow inside the burning building. Alice Spencer had gone into a burning building to get her out. Alice, who was terrified of fire and dark spaces.

Hannah's legs started moving towards the building.

Lucy grabbed her. "No, you mustn't."

"Let go of me, Lucy." Hannah fought against her.

Lucy grabbed her a little tighter, but Hannah was strong and started dragging Lucy behind her. A moment later, two other teachers were grabbing her and holding her in place. She fought against them, desperate to get free.

"Let me go! My daughter is in there!" she screamed.

27

AN UNLIKELY RESCUER

ALICE WAS in the building before she had time to think about what she was doing. The main downstairs corridor was completely filled with smoke. Thankfully, the thick, black smoke was confined to the ceiling, with a thinner mist at eye level.

The alarm bell screeched loudly so that she couldn't hear anything but the siren echoing down the hallway. She couldn't imagine how terrified Rosie felt. She had to get to her. And then kill Colin Whittaker.

She moved quickly, crouching low as she went. She turned and walked down a side corridor. She paused and looked around. It was the wrong direction. She'd only just entered the building, and she was already getting confused and turned around by the amount of smoke and her mounting fear.

She hurried in the right direction. The smoke was much thicker as she approached the library. In the distance she could see orange light flickering against a wall, an indication that the fire was just around the corner.

She paused again, staring at the eerie, amber glow that reflected off the walls. Her heartbeat sounded so loudly in her ears that she could no longer hear the alarm. She wondered if she was about to pass out. She'd experienced panic attacks before. This felt like her strongest one ever.

She reached out and held onto the wall, trying to find something solid that would ground her.

Rosie, get to Rosie, she told herself.

The sweet girl's smile appeared in her mind, and she pushed herself away from the wall. A few minutes later she entered the library. Already there was smoke filling the space, but it wasn't quite as bad as in the corridor.

She closed the door, hoping that it would buy them a little more time and a little more air before they headed back into the ever-darkening hallway.

There were three store cupboards in the room. Thankfully they all permanently had keys in their locks. She unlocked the first and threw the door open. It was completely empty.

She rushed around the shelving to the next door and struggled a few seconds with the lock before opening the door. She couldn't see anything and wondered if this was another of Colin's tricks. Maybe Rosie was outside, safe and well while she was in danger of being overcome by smoke in an empty library.

She was about to turn away to the third and final cupboard when she saw something.

"Rosie?"

She heard a noise. A cry.

She walked into the cupboard and could see Rosie

curled up in a ball at the back. She pulled the young girl into a strong embrace.

"Oh, Rosie, you're going to be okay," she promised, even though by now she was sure they were both going to perish. Rosie wasn't able to stand so she lifted her into her arms.

"Are you okay?" Alice asked, unsure if Rosie had already inhaled too much smoke.

"Are we going to die, Miss Spencer?" Rosie whispered.

"No, everything will be fine. The fire brigade are already on their way."

Alice walked into the library. Emergency lighting dully lit the windowless room. The only way out was the way she had come in, through the corridor.

She looked through the half-glazed door and was alarmed that she could no longer see through the smoke which had become much thicker and darker since she had arrived. She held Rosie tightly, trying to soothe the girl and her own thundering heart.

She didn't know what to do for the best.

The corridor looked impassable.

They'd have to run, and she didn't think Rosie could. She'd have to carry her, but it was a long way. She didn't know if she had the lung capacity to do so without being able to take a breath. There was a real chance that they'd be overcome by fumes in the hallway, which would mean certain death.

Her only chance was that the fire brigade had arrived and would be able to get to them. She congratulated herself on shouting to Lucy where she was going and why.

People knew where they were. Now it was just a matter of *when* they would arrive.

"Miss Spencer?" Rosie asked.

Alice knew that her indecision was costing them valuable time.

"I think we should stay here, Rosie," she said. "Let the fire brigade come for us."

She spun around and sat Rosie on the librarian's desk. She ripped off her jacket and her cardigan and put them under the door to try to stem the smoke that was pouring in.

She turned to Rosie. "Arms up," she instructed.

Rosie did what she was told, in between hacking coughs.

Alice pulled her school jumper off and plugged the remaining gap with it.

She looked at the door and realised there was nothing else she could do. Even being close to the door was causing her breathing to become strained.

"Come on." She picked Rosie up and carried her to the farthest corner of the room. She knew now it was all about giving them every extra second. She lowered Rosie to the floor by the wall and sat behind her, pulling her into a hug.

"It will be okay, Rosie. They are coming for us."

Rosie clutched her arms around her. "I'm sorry. I shouldn't have come to the library without permission."

"It's okay," Alice told her. She squeezed her a little tighter.

"Colin didn't believe there was another book in his series, so I wanted to show him," she explained. "He doesn't like being wrong. He was being silly. I told him to stop and then he—"

"Shh, don't worry about that now." Alice softly rocked her. She knew they needed to conserve oxygen and not waste the last few valuable molecules of breathable air talking about Colin. She turned Rosie around so her head rested against her chest. She unbuttoned her shirt and used the material as a mask, placing it over Rosie's mouth and nose.

"We'll be out soon," she promised, not knowing how much truth lay in the statement.

28

ANSWERS

SEVERAL PEOPLE HAD HELD Hannah back right up until the fire officers *finally* entered the building. Once she saw them march in with all their equipment, her body finally relaxed.

She was still beside herself with worry, but at least she now knew that something was happening. Lucy remained beside her, an arm wrapped around her in a useless attempt at comfort.

Hannah shook her head. She couldn't think like that. Lucy was doing her best. They'd never seen eye to eye, as it was between Hannah and most of Fairlight's residents. Especially anyone who was connected to her by this vile building.

She got her phone out of her pocket and rang Alice's mobile. She knew it was unlikely to yield any results, but if there was even a one percent chance she could hear that voice again, she'd take it.

The generic voicemail message sounded on the fifth ring, and Hannah sobbed.

"They'll be okay," Lucy told her. Her arm tightened. "Alice won't rest until she's found Rosie. She loves that girl."

Hannah briefly wondered if she'd told Rosie that she loved her enough. She thought she had, but now that the crunch had come, she couldn't be sure. Were there ever enough times to tell someone you loved them? She couldn't even remember saying goodbye to her that morning. And Adrian had dropped her off at school, all because Hannah was petty and argumentative. She'd missed the chance to spend a few more precious minutes with her daughter.

And Alice. She wished she hadn't been quite so harsh with her. She had been angry, but she knew she went off like a firecracker as she so frequently did when it came to protecting Rosie. Now, staring at the smoke streaming from the building, she wished she'd reacted differently.

"Miss Hall."

She looked up to see Hardaker walking towards her, a grim stare on his face. She had nothing to say to him.

"I assure you that everything is being done to ensure young Rose is brought out safely. Miss Spencer will have found her and be working with the fire service to bring her to safety," he explained to her.

She knew he had no idea what was going on and was just trying to keep her calm. She didn't have it in her to argue with him.

"I promise you, in no time at all Rosie will be back in her classroom wired up to Prince's Academy as if nothing had ever happened."

She tore her eyes away from the burning building. "What do you mean?"

"The placement she has," Hardaker explained. "For the online course for gifted pupils."

Hannah stared at him.

"Miss Spencer used her contacts to get Rosie a place at Prince's. Quite ingenious, students all over the country can learn via a laptop and the internet, being taught by the best with a view to those students attending Prince's when they are older. I'm sure Miss Spencer was going to explain it to you soon."

"She even got Mr Hardaker to open the kitty for a laptop," Lucy added.

"Well, she blackmailed me, if that's what you mean." Hardaker chuckled. "She's bloody-minded. Don't you worry, Miss Hall, your daughter couldn't be in safer hands."

Hannah felt sick.

She'd jumped to the conclusion that Alice was planning to send Rosie away, when she'd actually gone to the trouble of constructing the perfect scenario for Rosie. She could stay in her class but still have access to the education she needed.

Her body shook with shock.

She'd pushed Alice away, without giving her a chance to explain. She'd ended things because of a misunderstanding. As usual, Hannah Hall had gone defensive and shot herself in the foot.

"There's Rosie!" Lucy called out.

Hannah ripped herself away from Lucy and ran towards the fireman who had Rosie cradled in his arms.

He was walking towards an ambulance which had arrived shortly after the fire service. A paramedic was on standby beside a stretcher.

The fireman lowered her daughter onto the stretcher, and the paramedic quickly took over. The officer opened his visor and looked at Hannah.

"She's going to be okay," he said.

"Thank you! Thank you so much!" She looked at Rosie who was covered in soot and coughing but seemed strong and healthy.

She cried with relief and took her hand. "Hey, pumpkin, you're going to be okay." She turned and looked towards the school. No one else was coming out.

The paramedic was speaking to Rosie, asking her questions and cleaning her up, but the sound of her voice faded into the background as Hannah stared at the door, wishing for it to open and for Alice to walk out.

She started to hope that maybe Alice was already out. Maybe she hadn't been able to get into the building and was somewhere in the crowded playground.

"Some smoke inhalation that will need to be monitored, but she'll be fine," the paramedic was explaining.

"Where's Miss Spencer?" Rosie asked tiredly. "She was with me."

Hannah's heart sank.

"I… I don't know," she admitted.

She looked around the playground. More and more parents were turning up and taking their children away from the school. She wished she was one of them. Arriving and feeling the relief that your child was safe and well, taking them home and holding them tightly.

"She saved me," Rosie whispered.

Hannah squeezed her hand. She had nothing to say. She wished she could offer some comfort, but at that moment she was all out of positive thoughts.

The doors opened, cracking loudly on the walls on either side of them as a fireman pushed them aside. He held a limp body in his arms.

Alice, Hannah recognised her immediately.

In that moment, her heart stopped. It was only Rosie's hand squeezing her that brought her back from the dark void.

The fireman rushed to a stretcher and gently lowered Alice down, shouting information at the paramedic as he did.

"Mummy?" Rosie sounded terrified. She may have been facing away from what was happening, but she had picked up on the charge in the atmosphere. Parents and students in the distance were gasping and murmuring, the sound carrying easily across the now deathly silent playground.

Hannah stretched her neck to see what was happening. Alice was covered in soot, her eyes firmly closed. She looked like she was in a deep sleep, and Hannah refused to believe any differently.

"Mummy?" Rosie said again, this time more forcefully.

Hannah spun around and took Rosie into her arms, using her body as a shield so that Rosie wouldn't be able to see the paramedic working on her teacher.

"It's okay," she whispered. "It's okay."

She clung to Rosie, hoping to anyone who would listen that it really would be okay.

29

A FRIGHT

ALICE FOUGHT against the exhaustion to try to open her eyes. She couldn't remember anything. Something was clawing at her mind, telling her to wake up, to get up. Urgency tore through her, but she didn't know why.

In a flash, she remembered the fire, the library, and Rosie.

Her eyes opened. She tried to sit up but was unable to move very far.

"Whoa, whoa, calm down," a voice said. "You're okay. You're okay."

Someone had gripped her arm and was trying to get her to lie still.

"Rosie," she said, surprised to hear that her voice was a harsh rasp. She turned to see who was holding her back from getting to Rosie and was surprised to see that it was Hannah.

"Rosie is fine," Hannah reassured her. She sat on the edge of the bed, where its railings ended, the first indication to Alice that she was in hospital.

Alice shook her head. Rosie was in danger, and she needed to get to her.

Hannah gently pushed her back down and stood up, gesturing behind her to where Rosie sat asleep in a high-backed chair, Hannah's coat draped over her.

"She's?" Alice asked, struggling to think in full sentences, never mind speak them.

"She's absolutely fine. Thanks to you."

Alice sighed in relief without thinking. It caused her to cough, which, in turn, caused a painful ache in her chest.

Hannah picked up a cup of water with a small straw and held it out for her. She eagerly drank, hoping to rid her mouth and throat of the foul taste there.

"You gave us all a fright," Hannah said seriously.

Alice finished with the water, and Hannah put the cup back on the bedside table.

"I'm sorry, I didn't mean to," Alice apologised. "I, I don't remember much of it."

"That's okay. It's etched in my mind *forever*," Hannah said. "The woman who is scared of the dark and of fire ran into a burning building to save my daughter."

Alice couldn't believe it. She knew she'd done it, and she'd do it again in a second. But she still couldn't actually believe her actions. She looked at Rosie, safely tucked up asleep and knew she'd made the right decision. Even if she had, presumably, nearly died.

"The doctor wants to keep you in overnight to keep an eye on you. Pretty bad smoke inhalation, he said," Hannah explained.

Guilt washed over her and threatened to push her back

into a murky unconsciousness. "I'm sorry," Alice whispered.

Hannah looked at her as if she had grown another head. "What for?"

"For Rosie being in there. I should have been looking after her." Alice couldn't believe that she'd been standing in the playground sipping coffee and chatting with Lucy while a fire had started taking hold of the building and Colin and Rosie were roaming the library.

"Don't be ridiculous. Kids do dumb shit. Trust me, I did tons of stuff. You can't be expected to watch every child all the time. And, beyond that, you nearly died trying to save her." Tears fell down Hannah's cheeks. "I will never be able to thank you enough for saving my little girl."

"It's my fault," Alice repeated.

"No, it isn't," Hannah said firmly. "You did nothing wrong. In fact, you're a hero."

Alice tried to laugh, but it hurt. "I'm not," she argued. Her eyelids were starting to feel heavy.

"You are. Now, stop arguing. You're supposed to be resting."

Alice could feel herself fading. She didn't know if it was exhaustion or painkillers, but she didn't want to go just yet. She feared that when she woke up, Hannah wouldn't be there, and she needed to talk to her. Needed to explain.

Hannah seemed to sense her impending unconsciousness and perched on the edge of the bed, one hand holding hers and the other running fingers through her hair.

Her last thought before she drifted off was that her hair must have been disgusting.

30

PART OF A FAMILY

HANNAH SOFTLY CLOSED the hospital room's door behind her. She held Rosie in her arms, the dozing girl still not fully awake.

She wished she could have properly spoken to Alice. There were so many things that needed to be said. But it was the wrong time. Alice was disorientated and exhausted, and it was so late that Rosie needed to be in bed, not slumped in a hospital chair. Hannah decided she'd come back as soon as was practical and issue a grovelling apology.

"How is she?"

Hannah jumped a little. Lucy Gibson walked down the corridor towards her.

"She's asleep. She woke up for a few moments, but she's exhausted," Hannah explained. "I better get going."

She tried to sidestep Lucy.

"Wait a second." The woman put her hands up to stop Hannah from getting past.

"What do you want?" Hannah levelled her with a death glare.

"For this to end," Lucy said simply.

Hannah adjusted her grip on Rosie and let out a sigh. She didn't want to do this now. It was late. Everyone was tired and emotional.

"What do you mean?" Hannah asked. She suspected that she knew what Lucy meant, but she wasn't about to embarrass herself by making another assumption.

"This… whatever it is. You separate yourself from everyone in Fairlight. I know things have been hard for you—"

Hannah scoffed. "Are you kidding me? Of course, I keep to myself. You all hate me. I hear the gossip!"

"Everyone gossips about everyone," Lucy said. "You're not special or unique. And I know your life has been crap, and I know you have a problem when it comes to most people in town, my sister included, and I know it's well-deserved. But this isn't school anymore. We're all adults. People try to reach out to you, but you push them away. That needs to change, for her." Lucy gestured her head towards Rosie.

"Why bring this up now?"

"Because I have you trapped in a corridor," Lucy said. "You avoid me all the time. I don't get a chance to even say hello to you. We're not against you, Hannah. A lot happened in the past, but it is in the past. If you don't want to forgive your ex-classmates, I get that, but there are a lot of us who want you to be a part of our community. We nearly lost people today. There aren't many of us in

Fairlight, and I know you don't feel you're a part of it, but you are. Whether you like it or not."

Hannah opened and then closed her mouth. She wanted to argue, wanted to fight Lucy's calm words, but she couldn't. In her heart, she knew that Lucy Gibson had never actually done anything to her. She was just a member of the larger Fairlight community which she generally disliked.

Her dad had always accused her of having a chip on her shoulder. She denied it, of course, but she knew he was right. She'd decided many years ago that it was better to be alone than to give people the power to hurt her.

"I knew something was going on between you and Alice," Lucy whispered. "She'd been seen going into your apartment."

Hannah rolled her eyes. She bet that bit of information had spread quickly.

"Gossip. I know we're all terrible for it. But do you know what people were saying?" Lucy asked.

"Do I *want* to know?"

"They were saying you made a cute couple. They were saying how good Alice is with kids and how lucky Rosie would be to have her in her life. People want you to be happy, Hannah. As difficult as that may be to believe."

Hannah blinked. She'd assumed that any gossip about her would have been negative. She chuckled and shook her head. "Well, I messed it up, so you can report that back to everyone. Hannah Hall will be alone again."

"What happened?" Lucy looked genuinely interested.

"I made a mistake," Hannah confessed. "I saw a leaflet

for Prince's and assumed Alice wanted to send Rosie there."

"Oh." Lucy nodded. "Easy mistake to make. She didn't correct you?"

"I didn't give her much chance. I was typical me, jumped to conclusions, got mad, stormed out."

"Sounds like you," Lucy agreed.

"Hey," Hannah argued, but it lacked bite even to her ears. She recalled the fight, and something occurred to her. "Shit. The classroom."

"What?"

"She'd just finished breaking her back decorating the classroom. It's going to be destroyed now."

"I did a walk around the building a few hours ago," Lucy said. "Three classrooms are completely gutted, the rest is smoke damage. It's amazing that more wasn't ruined. We've called in a company to clean up."

Hannah felt angry. "She worked so hard, then nearly got herself killed. And now the classroom will be back to the shit state it was in before."

"Then do something about it," Lucy said.

"What? You expect me to repaint it?"

"Think bigger, Hannah. I'm trying to tell you that you are a member of this very small, very active community. I know you don't believe me, but it's true. Whether or not you want to be, you're part of the family, and family pulls together in times like this."

"You expect me to ask people to help?" Hannah stared at Lucy as if she'd suggested the most ridiculous thing in the world.

"Why not?"

"Because, as I might have mentioned, everyone hates me."

"And I'm trying to tell you they don't. You're caught up in the past, Hannah. Everyone else has moved on and wonders why *you* hate *them*. Why don't you test my theory and see if they really do hate you by trying to do something nice for Alice? What do you have to lose?"

Hannah thought about it for a moment. Maybe Lucy was right. Maybe she could encourage some people to help her out. Nearly everyone in town had attended the school or had children who had.

"Fine. I'll try and reach out to a couple of people," Hannah agreed. Part of her was certain that it wouldn't work out and that she'd be shunned, but she reasoned that then she could prove to Lucy that she was right.

Lucy pulled out her phone. "Cool, give me your number. We're going to need to stay in touch to organise this."

31

PULLING TOGETHER

HANNAH STOOD by the reception desk at Chopz, feeling frazzled.

"Okay, you're taking Rosie home to feed her and put her to bed," she explained to Adrian, more for her benefit than his. "I've got that delivery coming in twenty minutes which should be all the wood that John and Tim need. The Women's Institute ladies are bringing food for everyone, and they might work on the curtains if that delivery arrived this afternoon. I've got my clipboard. What else?"

Adrian sat in one of the salon chairs staring at her blankly. "I don't know. Do I need to salute you?"

"Oh, shut up," she told him.

A knock on the glass window got her attention, and she turned around. Mick and David waved at her and held up pots of paint. She opened the door.

"They donated? That's amazing!"

Mick nodded. "That's not all. They called their head office, and they want to help as well. They are sending paint and some of their employees to come and help tomorrow morning. I spoke with Lucy. She's going to be there to let them in and show them what to do."

"Great job," Hannah said. "That's a job off my list! I'm finishing up here, and then I'll join you."

The men said goodbye and continued their walk towards the school.

Hannah went back into the salon. "Did you hear that? I asked them to go to the hardware store on Mill Lane, and they get paint from a big supplier. I thought they might want to donate, and they did!"

"I can't believe how many people you have convinced to donate stuff," Adrian said. "Think you could speak to the travel agent about getting me a holiday?"

She ignored the quip. "Everyone wants to help the school. And Alice is a local hero now, so everyone wants to give back for her."

"Isn't she leaving hospital soon?"

"Tomorrow. Lucy has been visiting her, but I've been too busy. And if I take Miss Mouthy with me, then she'll spill the beans." Hannah gestured towards the staff room where Rosie was reading.

"You call your own daughter mouthy?" Adrian laughed.

"She can't keep a secret," Hannah said. She picked up her clipboard and swiped through a few pages to scrub paint from her list. "I'm planning to visit Alice at the weekend. Hopefully she'll be okay to see me and won't send me away."

Hannah still hadn't had a chance to speak with Alice since the few minutes in the hospital two days before. She didn't know if she would be welcome. Besides, she was busy single-handedly arranging for the school to be renovated.

Hardaker had had the insurance company come in. They'd cleaned whatever could be cleaned and threw away everything that was too smoke-damaged, but the school's insurance policy was basic to say the least.

Hannah had spoken to a couple of parents she knew reasonably well and tested the waters to see if they would be willing to donate time or money to helping with repairs. She'd been surprised by how receptive to the idea they'd been. Everyone was happy to help, even saying they would speak with friends, family, and employers to get more assistance.

Within a few hours, Hannah's phone had exploded with offers of help, and she'd become the main organiser of the clean-up effort. Donations of money, time, expertise, and materials were coming in from all over the place.

In between client appointments, Hannah had worked with a couple of the other mums to create a battle plan. They had lists of rooms to be cleaned, furniture to be replaced, and books to be catalogued. Every time Hannah turned around, she was face to face with a new volunteer eager and smiling.

Lucy had been right. Fairlight was a family. Hannah had just shut herself off from that. She'd taken her experiences at school and used them to shape her adult life.

Once she had taken the risk and reached out to people, she was shocked that they had responded positively. It wasn't just for the school, or for Alice. Hannah had spoken at length with people she was convinced hated her. She'd spent an hour the previous evening handing tools to Kevin, an electrician she had gone to school with. They'd chatted like old friends as he slowly repaired the Victorian fuses that had caused the fire to begin with.

People were starting to interact with Hannah more. She didn't detect any undertone to their behaviour, just a willingness to help. At first, she had thought that people were banding together because it was for the school, but she soon realised it was more than that. She'd had countless invites to events, dinners, and drinks at the local pub.

The Fairlight family seemed to be opening their collective arms to her.

It felt good. Scary, but good.

"She'll forgive you," Adrian said.

"I don't know how you can be so sure about that," Hannah replied, not looking up from her clipboard.

"Because you'll grovel. And you'll explain."

"What if that's not enough?" Hannah asked.

The door to the salon opened. She turned around and smiled when she saw Kath from the church choir. Kath had become her second in command.

"I was telling my son, Rob, about what had happened the other night. He owns a carpentry firm up in Yorkshire. Well, he's only gone and closed the company for the next few days, driven down here with his boys, and is going to build whatever we want! Cupboards, desks, doors... you name it!"

Hannah's jaw dropped open. "You're kidding."

"Nope. I told him we'd heard from the local wood merchant and they'd give us whatever we needed. He said he'd take them up on that offer. He's worked with primary schools in the past and has built beautiful spaces. I'm going to get my sewing group together. I thought we'd make some cushions and curtains for the youngsters' room. Nice and bright!"

Hannah's mind was spinning. Every time someone new showed up with some materials or expertise, the renovation plans grew a little. It was a wonderful problem to have, but the prospect of having a team of carpenters who had worked with primary schools in the past was game-changing.

Kath let out a sigh. "I'm no further with paint, though. I called up a couple of suppliers, but I couldn't get anywhere."

"Ah, Mick's just told me that we have a lot of paint coming from the hardware store," Hannah explained.

Kath's face lit up. "That's good news! Rob is bringing some pictures of things they've built before, to give us some ideas. Miss Spencer will be so surprised when she sees her new classroom!"

"She will, but remember, we need to keep it quiet," Hannah told her. "I know how news spreads in this town!"

"Absolutely! Everyone at the hospital knows to not say a word. And Lucy will be taking her home tomorrow. Then we just need to make sure she doesn't hear it around town for a few days." Kath looked at her watch. "I better get down to the school. Margaret is setting up the table for the hot food, and she's recently had laser eye surgery. She won't tell anyone, but it went a bit wrong. Anyway, I'll tell you all about it later."

Kath waved goodbye to Adrian and hurried off.

Adrian gasped. "You're inside the gossip circle!"

"I am, and if you're not nice, I'll tell you what they say about you," Hannah joked.

"I'm proud of you."

She looked at him in confusion for a few moments. "You mean the school? It's a joint effort, I'm just getting people together, but the real wo—"

"No, not the school. I'm proud of you for being brave and talking to people and asking them for help. I know that must have been a big deal for you. But you did it. And you've made friends."

She shook her head and looked away. "People are just helping out for the school. It's nothing to do with me."

"That's not true, and you know it. You asked for help, and people rallied round."

Hannah waved her hand to stop him from talking. She didn't want to have a conversation that would probably lead to her crying. It had been terrifying to reach out to people, but within a short space of time she'd gone from feeling like an outsider to a central component in the weird mix that made Fairlight.

"I have to go," she said. "You've got Rosie's bag? And you know you have to make her eat vegetables. I've been so rushed lately that I've been letting that slip. She needs to grow, or she'll be the shortest university graduate ever."

Adrian sighed, obviously fed up with being told the same information for the sixth or even seventh time.

"I'm going, I'm going!" She grabbed her things and started to make her way towards the school and her army of volunteers.

32

HOME

"Are you looking forward to going home?" the nurse asked as she hurried around the room, opening the curtains and writing something down on a clipboard.

"I'll miss you, but yes," Alice admitted.

An overnight stayed had turned into two overnight stays due to the doctor not being happy with her progress. Whatever that meant. Alice was ecstatic with her progress. She was alive, which was more than she had expected after running into the smoke-filled corridor.

Alice privately admitted to herself that she felt like she had been hit by a bus, but she also knew that the only thing that would make her feel any better would be to go home. She longed for her own bed and to not be constantly interrupted by nurses doing various tasks.

Her lungs felt sore, and her entire chest felt as though it had been compressed in a tight vice, but she felt better than she had when she'd first woken up. Her recovery was going in the right direction.

"Remember, you're signed off for a week," the nurse told her. "Definitely no work."

"I'll take it easy," Alice reassured her.

She wasn't looking forward to a week at home. She'd never been that great at filling time. Work was her life. If she wasn't marking schoolwork, she was prepping lesson plans. Her evenings were often filled with work, not because she enjoyed it, but because she didn't know how else to fill them.

She could only watch so much television before her eyes started to ache and she longed for some silence. Living alone was great in that you could do whatever you wanted, whenever you wanted, but it was also boring.

She thought back fondly to the evenings she'd spent with Hannah and Rosie. They'd talked and laughed for hours, with never a dull moment.

Alice frowned. Hannah hadn't been back to the hospital, and Alice didn't know what that meant. Hopefully that she was busy with work and nothing more sinister. She wanted to talk to her, explain everything, and suggest they try again.

Of course, Hannah needed to do something about her tendency to assume the worst. And Alice needed her to understand that she couldn't be judged solely upon the fact she had attended a boarding school herself.

There was a lot to discuss, but so far, there had been no opportunity to do so.

The door opened. Alice wondered if she'd be lucky enough to see Hannah step over the threshold at the exact moment she was thinking about her.

"Only me," Lucy greeted.

Alice tried not to look disappointed. "Hello, are you here to break me out?"

Lucy had been to see her every day and had even offered to drive her home.

"I am. How are you feeling?"

"Much better." It was the same stock answer that she gave to anyone who asked. In truth, she felt terrible, but she knew it was nothing that time and rest wouldn't fix.

"How is Rosie doing?" She'd asked before, but she wanted to ask again, wanted to reassure herself that everything was fine. A few seconds' glimpse of the girl asleep in her hospital room hadn't been enough to keep her panic at bay.

"Fantastic. You'd never know she'd been in the building. Hannah said she's even sleeping through the night with no issues or nightmares. Kids are resilient." Lucy sat down. "Hannah said to tell you that she'll come and see you tomorrow, if that's all good with you?"

Alice nodded quickly. "Yes, that would be great."

"Are you sure you don't want me to call your parents?" Lucy asked again. "They might hear and be worried?"

Alice had already said no, but she hadn't felt strong enough to explain why.

"We haven't spoken for many years," Alice admitted. "I'm gay. They don't approve."

"Oh!" Lucy looked shocked. Alice didn't know if it was the banishment by her parents or the fact that she was gay that caused the reaction.

"I'm sorry your parents feel that way," Lucy said sadly. "We're a bit dated here in Fairlight, but everyone is very open and welcoming, so you'll have a new family in us."

The tight feeling in Alice's chest increased as her emotions threatened to bubble over.

"Thank you," she whispered.

Throughout her life she'd encountered all kind of reactions to her sexuality, but the first people she'd come out to had been her parents. The ongoing rift between them hurt her deeply and would most likely never be healed. They weren't about to change their minds, and she wasn't going to miraculously change who she was.

But knowing that some people accepted her without a second thought, that still made her emotional. How could strangers be so kind when flesh and blood were so cruel?

"I thought I'd drop you off at home, raid your cupboards to see what you need, and then pop to the shops for you. I have to get some groceries myself anyway. That way, you can stay in for a couple of days until you're feeling better."

"That's very kind." Alice shuffled to sit up a little. "How are things at school?"

"Hardaker's got some cleaners in. The damage isn't as bad as it looked at first. A couple of rooms are gutted, but everything is structurally sound. It'll be another week before we are back up and running."

"Do they know what started the fire yet?"

"The electrics in the cellar. Something sparked, hit the wooden door, and up it went." Lucy shook her head. "Hardaker will have some questions to answer about maintenance once everything is back to normal."

Alice hoped that Hardaker would be forced to retire. She didn't want his job, but she did want someone who actually cared about the children in the role. He wasn't a bad man, just lazy and ineffective. She'd never forgive his shoddy maintenance for almost killing Rosie.

"I need to speak to Colin Whittaker," Alice mumbled.

"I think he's grounded for a decade," Lucy said.

"That's not going to help him. The boy has issues. There's something deeper going on there."

"That's true, but that's for another day," Lucy said. She turned to the nurse who was still in the room, making notes on her clipboard. "Right. Who do we need to bribe to get her discharged?"

33

EXPLANATIONS

"You will tell her, won't you?" Rosie's pout was firmly set on her face.

"I will tell her. I promise."

"And you'll not forget to give her the drawing," Rosie added.

Hannah tapped her pocket. "I have the drawing right here. I won't forget."

Rosie blew out a long, hard done-by breath. "Why can't I go?"

Hannah crouched down and looked at Rosie seriously. "I know you want to see Miss Spencer, I understand that. But she's still recovering, and we have to have a serious conversation which would be very boring for you. Not to mention that I don't believe for one second that you'd be able to keep quiet about all the things happening at the school."

Rosie's eyes lit up. Hannah laughed and pointed at her face. "See? Right there, that's the face of someone who cannot keep a secret."

"I can!" Rosie proclaimed. "Sometimes."

"Okay, we'll work on your poker face, and maybe you can see her in a few days. But for now, I need to see her alone. And you'll have a great time helping Uncle Adrian out at school."

The doorbell rang, and Hannah let out a sigh of relief. She'd been building up to this moment for a while, knowing she couldn't avoid it. Of course, she wanted desperately to see Alice, but she also knew she had a lot of apologising to do, apologies which might not be accepted.

"Come on, pumpkin. Let's go." They walked down the stairs and out into the street. Adrian greeted them both, and they all climbed into his car.

"Nervous?" he asked quietly as they drove towards Alice's house.

"Yep." She popped the *p*.

"You'll be fine."

He'd been telling her that all along. She wasn't sure how he had come to that conclusion. He didn't know Alice, hadn't been there for the fight. And yet, somehow, he felt sure that everything would be okay.

Or he was just saying that in order to keep her calm.

Most likely the latter.

"This is the address," he said as they pulled up to a small cottage on the edge of town.

"Be good," she called out as she opened the car door.

"She's always good," Adrian told her.

"She was talking about you," Rosie informed him.

"She's right. Love you, pumpkin!" She closed the door and walked up the small pathway to the door. Her legs felt like concrete.

She heard the car drive away and felt suddenly alone and terrified. She wanted to turn around and run away. She didn't want to hear Alice tell her once and for all that their burgeoning relationship was over.

The door opened before she had a chance to knock.

She must have looked shocked as Alice explained, "I saw you from the kitchen window. Come in."

Being invited in, good start, Hannah thought.

She stepped into the hallway. There were still some moving boxes in the corner, but it was cosy and quaint.

She took a deep breath and finally made eye contact with Alice. "How are you?" she asked. She looked better than she did at the hospital, but still ashen and not her usual self.

"Better," Alice said. "Not fully recovered, but I'm sure it won't be long. Can I get you a drink?"

Hannah shook her head. "I should be making you a drink, you're just out of hospital!" She brushed past Alice towards the kitchen, where she picked up the kettle from the counter and filled it with water.

Alice walked into the room, and Hannah gestured towards the dining area.

"You rest."

"I've been resting endlessly."

"Well, rest some more. I want to make you a drink. It will make me feel better." Hannah knew she could never repay Alice for what she had done. She also knew there was a very big chance that Alice wouldn't forgive her and that this would be the final time they spoke like this. It soothed her to keep busy, to be finding her way around an

unfamiliar kitchen and making drinks rather than twid-
dling her thumbs.

With a few instructions, Hannah made hot tea for
them both and then took a seat at the dining table. She
realised that her distraction was over and now she had to
speak. The air had to be cleared.

"Hannah, I need to explain," Alice started.

Hannah quickly shook her head. "I know about the
online course."

Alice looked confused. "You know?"

"Hardaker explained. After you'd gone into the
building and I was being held back from running in after
you. I felt so stupid. I can't believe what I said to you,
what I accused you of. You're fully within your rights to
never forgive me, but I wanted to try to explain and to
apologise."

Alice looked down at her mug. "Go on."

Hannah blew out a nervous breath. "I... I'm a loner.
Always have been. And I'm pretty much set to negative. I
always think something will go wrong. I make stupid
assumptions about people, their motivations, the weather,
you name it. But it gets worse when I *really* care."

Hannah shuffled nervously in her seat. "I'm used to it
just being me and Rosie against the whole world. I love
her so much that I just want to protect her from everything in a way I was never protected, but I realise I go too
far. I shelter her too much. And I'm always waiting for
something to go wrong.

"So, when you came into our lives, I was scared from
the first moment I spoke to you. Scared that you would
somehow upset the balance in our little world, scared that

you'd hurt Rosie or me or both of us. Not because I think you're a bad person, but because that's what I'm used to. Good things didn't really happen to me when I was growing up. I don't want to sit here and spin you a sob story, but things were rough, and it's always stuck with me."

Hannah threw her head back and looked at the ceiling for a couple of moments while she thought about what to say next. She lowered her head and looked sincerely at Alice.

"When I saw that leaflet it was like… almost relief that I'd found the thing that was wrong with you."

Alice chuckled.

"No, seriously," Hannah said. "I'd been waiting for you to say you didn't want to see me anymore, or for you to be married, or for something to come between us. I saw the leaflet, and it was like I'd found it, I found the thing that would end it all. No more waiting to see what would go wrong. No more worrying that it would come at a time when I'd become so close to you that it could break my heart."

Alice nodded in understanding but remained silent.

"I said some things I regret. I reacted like a child having a tantrum. I didn't give you a chance to explain. And for all of that I'm so, so sorry. I will understand if you don't want to see me again."

"What if I do want to see you again?" Alice asked calmly.

Hannah hadn't expected that. "I… well, that…"

"You see, I know we've not known each other for very long," Alice said, "but I've become very fond of you. And

Rosie, of course. And I don't think, personally, that it's worth ruining whatever this is over a simple misunderstanding."

Hannah could hear the blood rushing through her ears. She hadn't expected this. A second chance was being given to her, so freely and easily.

"I'd like that. No, actually, I'd love that," Hannah said honestly.

"You have to make some promises to me, though." Alice turned serious. "No more storming away. If we have a disagreement or a misunderstanding, we talk. I understand that you err towards the negative, and that's completely natural. Many people do. But I don't ever want you to walk away from me like that again, if you can help it."

"I'll try my best," Hannah agreed.

"I'm also at fault. I became upset by what you said and the assumptions you made. I could have easily put the brakes on that entire argument, but I didn't. I was hurt by your assumption about my own upbringing."

Hannah hung her head in shame. "I'm sorry."

"I need to explain something to you," Alice said.

Hannah looked up and waited, as Alice seemed to mentally prepare herself to speak.

"I knew I was gay when I was very young. With absolutely certainty from when I was old enough to understand anything about relationships and love. I just knew. And, after a few years of trying to figure out what it all meant, I told my parents that I was gay. The change in our family dynamic was immediate. Quite simply, my parents stopped loving me. I felt certain that it would change over time, but it didn't."

Hannah reached out and caught Alice's hand and held it tight.

"Years went by, not many, but enough to really cement that there was no loving relationship between us anymore. My grades were excellent, and I heard about the concept of boarding schools. I applied for information. The idea of getting away from my parents was the only light I had."

Alice twisted her hand around and grasped Hannah's.

"When my dad found the leaflets and asked if I wanted to go to boarding school, I said I did. And that was that. I was out of the house two weeks later. I didn't go home during school breaks. The other students and the teachers became my family. It's why I went into teaching. I never went back home."

Hannah felt sick to her stomach. The idea that a parent could eliminate their own child from their life based upon their choice of partner was beyond her comprehension. Nothing Rosie could ever do would stop her from loving her, no matter what path she took. It wouldn't be possible for her to not love her own DNA.

"I…" Hannah swallowed. "I'm *so* sorry."

"I know there is a stereotypical view of people who go to boarding school, and I know that my parents spent a lot of money to send me there. But it isn't like the media would have you believe. And, for me as well as for some of my friends, it was a haven away from terrible parents. Something I seem to think you have some understanding of?"

Hannah softly inclined her head. "Yes." She wasn't

ready to share that part of her story yet. "I'm sorry I jumped to conclusions and said what I said. I don't feel that way, not really. I was just being defensive. It's my biggest problem. I'm working on it, though."

"At least it comes from a place of love," Alice said, a smile starting to grace her face. "It's an admirable trait."

"Maybe a place of fear, too," Hannah confessed. "You... I was frightened by just how quickly you were becoming important to me." Hannah decided it was time to be bold and honest. If Alice wasn't on the same page, then it was better to know now.

Her answer came in the form of Alice's smile, which even met her twinkling eyes.

"I'm glad I'm not the only one to feel that way," Alice admitted. "I don't know what it is about you, Hannah Hall, but I just can't stop thinking about you."

Hannah's heart felt full to bursting. Maybe she hadn't ruined everything. Maybe there was a chance that she could have a happy ending with this wonderful woman in front of her.

"It's just so fast," Hannah said. "I got so scared."

"I've never felt like this before," Alice said, grasping Hannah's hand tighter and sitting a little closer. "And I understand your fear, really I do. You have Rosie to think of as well. And god, I love that little girl, and I love how much you love her. You're filled with love for each other, and it makes me so happy to see it. She's okay, isn't she? I know there must be some trauma. She was terrified, but—"

"She's good, she's bounced right back. I'm sure we'll have some nightmares and some such as she processes things, but all she's been talking about is you and wondering if you're okay." Reluctantly, she pulled her hand back and pulled the drawing out of her pocket. "She demanded I give you this."

Alice took the folded sheet of paper and slowly unravelled it. She snorted a laugh. "So, this…"

"Yep, that's you in a burning building with her. Doesn't it make you feel better?" Hannah laughed.

"It's… lovely?" Alice questioned before laughing again. She held a hand over her chest. "Oh, it hurts to laugh."

"I'm sorry." Hannah giggled and folded up the drawing. "I'll tell her you loved it, obviously."

"I appreciate the time and the effort, if not the final result. I don't think I ever want to be reminded about that again."

Hannah's hand shook and wedged it under her thigh. She hadn't even been in the building, but she was still terrified. She knew she had no right to be, not in comparison to what Alice had been through.

"I want to tell you to never do that again," Hannah confessed, "but if you hadn't, then… Rosie." A sob escaped her, and she quickly covered her mouth with her hand. "I'm sorry," she whispered.

Alice was on her feet in an instant, she leant over Hannah and wrapped her arms around her shoulders. "Don't be sorry. I can't imagine what it must have been like for you. Knowing that Rosie was in there and unable to do anything, it must have been terrifying."

Hannah took some calming breaths and got herself under control. She reminded herself that everything was fine, that all her darkest fears were just fears. Everyone was safe. She nodded, indicating that she was okay.

Alice took a step away. Hannah took her hand before she could get too far away. Alice looked hesitant, though, and gently tried to pull her hand away.

Hannah let her go. "Did I do something wrong?" she asked.

Alice crossed the kitchen. "No, not at all. It's just… I still smell of the fire. I think it's my hair. I can't get rid of the smell. I don't feel very attractive."

"Come by the salon as soon as you're feeling better. I'll sort that out for you. You'll be back to your usual sweet-smelling self."

Alice grinned. "I'd like that." She blushed. "How about tomorrow? Or is that too soon?"

Hannah returned the grin. "Tomorrow sounds perfect."

34

SURPRISE

ALICE GOT out of her car and they began the short walk to Hannah and Rosie's door. She noticed two people cross the road when they saw her. Maybe it was her imagination, but that seemed to have been happening all week.

She'd have been a little more concerned about it if she hadn't been so preoccupied by her company during the times it had happened. She'd managed to get some time with Hannah every single day of her week-long recovery period. From hair appointments to lunches, walks in the park, and dinner, she couldn't get enough of Hannah. She was happy to be on her way to another dinner, this time with Rosie, whom she hadn't seen at all.

If she were to guess, she'd have assumed that Hannah was trying to protect Rosie from their relationship while she decided whether they were likely to stay the course. There was no point in getting Rosie excited about them being an item if it looked like they wouldn't be one for long. The fact that she was now having dinner with

Hannah and Rosie made her heart soar at the possibility that Hannah had decided they were on more solid ground.

She raised her hand to ring the buzzer when the door flew open and Rosie rushed into her legs.

"Miss Spencer!" she screamed happily.

Alice was nearly bowled over by the enthusiastic hug. She recovered and rested her hands on Rosie's shoulders. When she looked up, she saw Hannah standing in the doorway with her coat on.

She frowned as she realised that Rosie was also wearing a coat, as well as a wool hat and thick scarf. It seemed like overkill for greeting someone at the door.

"Did I get my wires crossed? Are we going out for dinner?"

Hannah shook her head. "No. We're just heading somewhere else first."

She narrowed her eyes. "What are you up to?"

"You'll see." Hannah closed the front door. "Pumpkin, let Miss Spencer breathe."

Rosie reluctantly loosened her grip, but still leaned against Alice. She looked up. "I've missed you."

"And I've missed you," Alice said.

"We have a surprise to show you," Rosie said.

"Ahem," Hannah said loudly. "This is exactly why you haven't been able to see Miss Spencer this week."

Alice looked from Rosie's excited face to Hannah. "What's going on?"

Hannah took her arm and looped it through hers. "All in good time."

Rosie took her other hand, and they all walked down

the street. Alice noticed people were standing around, seemingly watching them.

"Are they staring at us?" Alice asked Hannah in a whisper.

"Yes, you'll see why soon."

Alice had no idea what Hannah meant by her cryptic comment, so she just enjoyed the walk through town with her two new favourite people. When it became clear that they were walking towards the school, she stopped dead.

"This isn't some awful welcome back thing, is it?"

Hannah shook her head. "No, that's Monday. I've told them to keep it short because I know you won't enjoy it. This is just the three of us. I have a key to the school."

"*You* have a key to the school?" Alice couldn't understand why anyone would give Hannah a key, nor why she would want one.

"Come on, Miss Spencer." Rosie dragged her towards the school, unable to put up with her hesitation any longer.

She allowed herself to be pulled along. She eyed the building as they walked down the road. It looked like nothing had ever happened. She knew that there hadn't been as much damage as she'd worried there would be due to the quick actions of the fire service, and it had been over a week since the incident. But it was still a surprise to see it looking so normal on the horizon.

They entered the playground, and Alice smiled.

"Oh, new doors?"

"Yes, new doors," Hannah agreed as she unlocked them. "The old ones were so heavy to open, and they got damaged."

"In the fire?" Alice frowned. The fire had been nowhere near the main entrance.

"In the clean-up, I'll explain later." Hannah opened the door and gestured for Rosie and Alice to step inside.

Rosie reached up and flipped on a multitude of switches on a new panel. Lights sprung to life.

Alice gasped. "New lights?"

"New electrics," Hannah said. "New wiring everywhere."

"That must have cost a lot," Alice mumbled as she looked down the corridor, remembering with hesitation the last time she'd stumbled down it.

"Not as much as you'd think," Hannah said. She opened the next set of doors and gestured for Alice to enter the first classroom.

Rosie pulled her along, dragging her into the room and gesturing dramatically.

Alice's mouth fell open in shock. The walls had been plastered over and painted, the furniture was new, and a series of brand new whiteboards were fixed to the wall. It looked like a new room entirely.

"This is amazing," Alice said as she looked around.

"This is nothing," Hannah told her. "This is just year six. Pfft. Boring. Let's go and see year one."

Alice spun around to look at her. "My classroom's been renovated?"

"You could say that." Hannah held out her hand. "Let's go check it out."

Alice took her hand and found herself being pulled towards the stairs. Rosie quickly overtook them and bounded up the stairs. Alice noticed that the stairwell had been repainted and the window frames had been fixed. There was no more splintered wood or flaking paint.

"Close your eyes," Rosie announced before they got to the room.

Alice laughed and closed her eyes.

"Mummy, is she looking?" she heard Rosie question.

She felt Hannah's body behind her and then her hands gently cover her eyes. "This will stop any cheating," Hannah said.

"I wasn't cheating!" Alice denied.

"Tell it to the judge," Hannah whispered in her ear. "Okay, lead the way, pumpkin."

Alice shuffled forward, being guided through the doorway by Hannah behind her. She could feel the energy and excitement bouncing off of Rosie and could even hear her heavy breathing.

"Open them!" the girl cried.

Hannah removed her hands, and Alice opened her eyes. She blinked. She turned her head and then spun her whole body around to check where she was. It felt like a trick. They couldn't possibly be in her classroom. It was unrecognisable.

"Wha—"

The floor had been replaced, the walls plastered and painted in bright colours, with a custom mural painted on one of them. She couldn't believe her eyes as she saw the bespoke desks and other furniture.

Rosie skipped across the room and into a cushioned area with seating, beanbag chairs, and shelves full of books.

"This is our new reading area!" Rosie exclaimed.

"A reading area?" Alice ran her hand along the shelves and then picked up and hugged one of the bright yellow cushions.

She spun around and saw a row of brightly painted coat hooks with each of her student's names written on them in calligraphy. Small boxes lay below to collect their winter wear.

It was the classroom of her dreams, somewhere that children would love to come and learn. Something else hit her like a brick.

"It's *warm*."

"Yeah, heating's fixed."

She turned and looked at Hannah in total shock. "How?"

She knew the school had called in on its insurance, but this was beyond what insurance could do. This was a full renovation and looked expensive.

"This is Fairlight coming together," Hannah said.

"But how?"

Hannah's cheeks reddened. "Me," she whispered.

"How?" Alice asked again.

"I told everyone how you'd been spending your own time and money painting the classroom. Told them that you nearly—" Hannah glanced at Rosie, who had picked up a book and was making full use of the reading area.

Hannah swallowed.

"I explained what you did. Everyone wanted to help. They called their friends, their employers. Before long there was a workforce of over a hundred people in here. They wanted to clean up the school, but they also wanted to make it safe and do something special for you. So, here is your special gift. The best classroom in Fairlight. Probably in the county."

Alice felt tears running down her cheeks. She couldn't believe that so many people had come together to do all of this work for free. And that Hannah had started it all.

"I've been in here every day. I have my own hard hat," Hannah explained. "It's why you couldn't see the munchkin. She would have spilt the beans in an instant, and I wanted to keep it a secret."

Alice was speechless as she looked around the room. Every sweep of her eyes uncovered something new.

"The windows have all been repaired. They're not new, but they don't let so much draft in now. Rotten window frames have been replaced. New electrics, new heating. Actually, a new boiler which was donated by this lovely man in town," Hannah continued. "And there's a new parent group that has been founded, we can keep on top of maintenance issues, so everything gets fixed. I'm the chairwoman, so, you know… if you need anything."

Alice wanted to launch herself into Hannah's arms and kiss her but knew she needed to hold back with Rosie in the room.

"I don't know what to say," she admitted.

"Well, think of something because on Monday there will be a full school assembly at the end of the day where you'll be applauded as the hero you are," Hannah said with a chuckle, knowing that Alice would hate every second of it.

She rolled her eyes. "Can I send a stunt double?"

Hannah shook her head. "No, the town wants to see you."

"Will you be there?" Alice asked, shyly.

"You won't be able to keep me away," Hannah said. "Anyway, come on, we need to go home and eat. I promised you dinner."

Alice looked at her room one last time before they made their way out of the school, turning off all the lights as they went. Rosie was running around the playground as Hannah locked the main front doors.

"Thank you so much for all of this," Alice said. "I'll have to think of a way to repay you." She ran her hand up Hannah's back suggestively.

Hannah chuckled. "On that note, Rosie seems to have picked up on the fact that we're dating. And literally everyone in town has been asking me when we're moving in together."

Alice removed her hand and stared at her. "Everyone knows?"

"Everyone," Hannah said.

"Do... do you want to pull back a little? Especially for Rosie's sake?" Alice asked, suddenly fearful of the answer.

"Not unless you do," Hannah said. "Usually the rumour mill bothers me, but a lot has happened since the fire, and me and Fairlight are getting on a little better. Rosie is over the moon and has promised to be good and not push us."

Alice swallowed. Her mind was stuck on the question of when they would move in together. She had to admit, she'd thought about it. She'd spent some of her recuperation week clearing out her spare room and thinking about where a bed would go. Not that she'd admit that to Hannah, it was much too soon.

Then again, most of their relationship seemed to be running at double speed. Things felt right.

"I'd like to continue as we are," Alice said, "but if you feel we do need to slow down, for Rosie's sake, then, of course, I will."

Hannah pocketed the keys and placed a soft kiss on Alice's lips. "Let's not change a thing."

35

A BUMPY START

OVER DINNER, Rosie spoke at length about all of the people who came out to help renovate the school. Hannah blushed while Rosie spoke about the donations and people she had organised with enormous pride.

After the meal, Rosie was suddenly keen to go to bed. She insisted on not having a bedtime story and told the adults to stay up and enjoy their evening. Alice had smothered a laugh behind her hand while Hannah had blushed bright red.

Despite her protests, Hannah put Rosie to bed. Alice cleaned the dinner plates away, not wanting to have a second with Hannah wasted by chores.

When Hannah returned, Alice had poured some drinks for them both and was sitting on the sofa grinning.

"Miss Matchmaker asleep?" she asked.

"I'm so sorry," Hannah said. "I told her not to push us and to just leave whatever will happen to happen. She thinks she's being subtle."

"It's cute," Alice reassured. "It would be a lot worse if she didn't approve."

Hannah sat next to her. "True. That would be *much* worse. At least at the moment she's trying to make herself scarce."

"While I appreciate the offer, tell her she doesn't need to," Alice said. "I want to spend time with both of you."

Hannah turned to face her head on. "You're perfect."

Alice laughed. "I'm really not. I have lots of terrible traits. I'm just keeping them all under wraps."

Hannah grinned and casually rested her head in her hand. "Like what?"

"I take far too long in the bathroom," Alice said. "I like to sleep with the hallway light on, so it isn't too dark. My music tastes are terrible. I'm the only person in Britain who hates reality television—"

"Not the only person."

"I've lived on my own for so long I'm probably terrible to live with," Alice continued. "I won't have a bad word said about my car."

"Oh, well, I'm afraid it's all over. Because your car is a trash heap," Hannah said.

Alice smacked her arm gently. "You *will* take that back."

"I won't. I've heard the gears crunch from two streets away."

"She doesn't like the cold weather," Alice defended.

"She? It has a name?"

"Of course, don't you name cars?"

"I've never had a car, but if I did, I don't think I'd have named it. What's the scrap metal called?"

Alice paused.

"Oh, it's good." Hannah leaned forward. "Go on, what is your Mini called?"

"Gertrude," Alice whispered.

Hannah fell about laughing. "Seriously? You call your car Gertrude? Do you *not* like it?"

"She looked like a Gertrude," Alice explained and then put her head in her hands. "Okay, enough talking about my car. I demand a change of topic." She looked up again.

Hannah's grin slowly started to fade. Alice could tell that they were about to have a very serious change of topic. Suddenly she wanted to return to talking about the name of her car.

"I..." Hannah trailed off. "You told me about your childhood, and I wanted to do the same, because it might explain a few things."

Alice licked her lips. "Okay, if you're ready? You don't have to. I'm happy to wait."

"I want to. If I don't tell you, then someone else might, and I want to be the one to explain."

Alice nodded and waited for Hannah to gather the courage to start her story. It took a few silent moments, so Alice tried to clear her mind of assumptions and wait to hear the truth directly from the source.

"I've always pushed people away," Hannah began. "Always. Potential partners, friends, the entire village. I wanted to be independent, didn't want to have to rely on other people because that never really worked out for me as a child.

"My dad was great, still is great. But he was never there. He'd leave for work for long periods of time and leave me with my mum. She wasn't so great, not that it was her fault. I supposed it would have been picked up by the council's mental health service if it happened now, but it wasn't."

Hannah reached for her wine glass and took a long sip.

"My mum had a lot of issues, but no one knew. She'd go into depressive states for days at a time. Sometimes she'd be fine, but most of the time she wasn't. And when we were at home, just the two of us, she tuned out. She didn't clean, cook, wash clothes… nothing."

Alice felt her blood run cold at the thought of Hannah growing up in such conditions.

"I often went to school hungry, didn't have a packed lunch with me. My uniform was often dirty and never ironed. Kids pick up on that kind of thing really quickly, and I was picked on. A lot. I was the dirty, scruffy kid. The one who stole from other people's lunchboxes when they weren't looking. I never had friends over, and I was seen around the village at all hours."

Alice reached out and took one of Hannah's hands in both of hers. She didn't know what to say. It was all in the past, it couldn't be fixed, but it must have had a massive effect in her.

"No one in this village did a thing to help me. I was bullied by the students and the teachers. I was in and out of Hardaker's office all the time. No one knew what was happening at home, and no one asked. And when my dad came home, my mum kind of snapped out of it. She said she'd not been feeling well and that's why the kitchen was a mess, things like that. It went on for years."

Alice grasped Hannah's hand tighter.

"Eventually, it all came out. She took a really bad turn and was walking the streets in her dressing gown. The authorities were called, and she was eventually institutionalised. My dad came home and looked after me for the last couple of years of school. I was off the rails by then, terrible grades, underage drinking, hanging out with the wrong crowd. I was the talk of Fairlight."

Hannah stopped and took a deep, shaky breath.

"Sorry, I've never really told anyone any of this before," she confessed. "Everyone around here knows. Well, they know their version of things."

"You don't need to apologise," Alice said. "Take your time."

"I was so angry at everyone for not noticing what was happening to me. At first, I was a kid and didn't know any better. Then I realised something was wrong, and I felt such *shame*. Like I was to blame, and I had to keep it quiet. By the time I realised something was wrong, I'd spent years being bullied and didn't want any more negative attention on me or my family."

Alice was starting to understand a lot of Hannah's demands for Rosie to have an ordinary school life. It must have been hellish for Hannah, growing up in a town where no one had noticed the terrible things she was going through on a daily basis. That kind of life left scars.

"Anyway, that was my childhood at Willows. I refused to ever step foot inside that place again after I finally left. It was only Rosie's appearance that changed that. I never left Fairlight, didn't know where else to go. Better the devil you know, right?"

Alice worried her lip. "May I ask about Rosie?"

"A club, too much to drink. Stupid stuff, really. Suddenly, I was pregnant. It shook me up, though, made me knuckle down and get myself sorted out. Spoke to Adrian, got a trade under my belt."

"And… the father?"

"No idea who he was," Hannah said with a sad grin. "Want to run away now?"

"I don't run," Alice said seriously.

Hannah slumped a little. "I'm sorry. I'm just defensive. I've had to learn to be that way, but I'm trying to be better. Trying to do better."

"That's all anyone can ask," Alice said. "And after all you've been through, it's no surprise that you're cautious. Anyone would be. But I'm not sure I understand. Why the sudden change? You said you've been getting on a little better with people after the fire?"

Hannah chuckled. "Yeah. Someone spoke to me and said I should try to reach out and see what happens rather than assuming the worst. So, I did, and I realised that I got a lot of people wrong."

"People were willing to help?"

"Yes. And people who I thought had a problem with me either didn't or thought I had a problem with them. And many people I went to school with seemed to have forgotten about everything that I remembered with crystal clarity. It's weird how something can be the most intense experience in your life while it's no more than a blip for other people. I realised I'd been keeping to myself and pushing everyone away. Typical Hannah. I did it as a child, and I was doing it as an adult."

"I'm really glad to hear that they surprised you, though I can't blame you for reacting the way you did. I'm sure a lot of people would have."

"Thank you." Hannah sat up and looked a little nervous. "I just wanted to explain this all to you so that you know what you're getting yourself into. I'm a bit messed up, but I'm trying fix it. I don't know if you're up for that?"

"I'm very much up for that," Alice said. "Your upbringing is obviously going to have an effect on your life, but it doesn't mean you're condemned to always feel that way. And I'd be proud to be with you while you figured things out. I like to think that we all spend our lives figuring things out, discovering new parts of our personality and working to change them."

"Yeah, like you once thought calling a car Gertrude was a great idea," Hannah sassed.

"That's it!" Alice launched herself onto Hannah and tickled her. She knew that Hannah had had enough of being serious, and the joke was her way of breaking the tension. Alice was only too pleased to help her with that.

Hannah was stronger than Alice and quickly managed to gain control, seizing both of Alice's thin wrists in one hand and using the other to attack her ribs.

Alice tried her best to keep quiet, knowing that Rosie was asleep next door. She decided attack would be the best form of defence and kissed Hannah squarely on the mouth. It worked. Hannah was distracted enough to release Alice's hands.

She considered using her freedom to attack Hannah

again but decided against that course of action as the kiss increased in intensity. Instead, she wrapped her arms around Hannah, pulling her close.

Hannah tore her lips away and started pressing small kisses down Alice's jawline. "I wish you could stay over," she murmured.

"I have a spare room," Alice whispered. "Maybe you could come to mine. Rosie can have the spare room, and you can come in with me. Might not be as comfortable as this sofa, though."

Hannah nipped her ear with her teeth as punishment for the jibe. "I'd like that," she admitted.

"We'll arrange dinner, slowly get Rosie used to my place and see how she feels about staying over one night," Alice suggested.

Hannah pulled away and stared into her eyes. "You really are perfect."

It was said with such conviction and strength that Alice was momentarily stunned.

"I—I feel the same about you, both of you," she confessed when she finally got her voice back. "In fact, I know some people have trouble saying it, but I've never had a problem with telling people how I feel. Even if it means the L word."

Hannah grinned. "I *like* you, too."

Alice rolled her eyes. "You know what I mean," she argued softly.

Hannah took her face in her hands. "Alice, I've fallen in love with you," Hannah said seriously.

Alice's breath caught in her lungs, prevented from

escape as her heart grew eight times bigger. She could barely hold back a squeal of excitement as she pulled Hannah into a rib-crushing hug.

36

COLIN

ALICE WALKED around the playground at afternoon break on her first day back at work. Apparently nearly dying didn't get anyone off of the playground duty roster. Children were running around, and everything looked like any other day, even though she knew it wasn't.

It had all started with a strange morning. Her students had hugged her and given her a welcome back card. It had taken a long time to get them all calm and settled for lessons. This was probably not helped by the fact that her own mind was distracted.

She kept thinking about the full school assembly that was happening at the end of the day. Everyone would be there, even the photographer from the local newspaper. She didn't like the fuss. She'd asked Hannah to try to cancel the whole event, but Hannah claimed it was out of her hands.

Apparently, everyone wanted to see her and thank her. Alice shivered at the very idea.

"Miss Spencer?"

She turned around and saw a boy she didn't recognise, someone from year two or three.

"Yes?"

"When you were in the fire, did you use an axe to break down the doors?"

Another boy appeared. "Yeah, and did you have to leap over holes where the floor had given out?"

"Yes," she said simply. "All of that."

"Cool!" The boys ran off to tell their friends.

She didn't want to tell them that she spent most of it huddled in a corner of the library expecting to die. Their parents probably wouldn't want her telling them that either.

"There's the hero!" She heard Hannah's voice.

She turned around to tell her off for announcing such nonsense so loudly in a public area but stopped dead when she saw an older man walking into the playground beside Hannah.

"Alice Spencer, this is Jon Hall, my dad," Hannah introduced. "Who decided to turn up out of the blue this morning."

Jon chuckled. "She's telling me off, can you tell?"

Alice swallowed nervously. She hadn't expected to meet Hannah's father, and she wondered if she looked presentable.

She held out her hand. He looked at it and laughed loudly as he brushed it to one side. Instead he held out his arms and pulled her into a gentle bear hug.

"Thank you for saving my granddaughter," he said. He stood back and looked into her eyes. "And for making my daughter happier than I've seen her in a long time."

"I, um, it's lovely to meet you," Alice replied, not sure what else to say.

"You're frightening her, Dad," Hannah said. She looked at Alice. "He's a big teddy bear, don't worry."

Big was right. Jon Hall was extremely tall and well built. His smile was kind, like Hannah's.

"I hear these lot are going to embarrass you with some presentation?" Jon asked, ignoring Hannah.

"Yes, unfortunately," Alice said. "I'd rather get back to work and forget about it."

Jon tutted and shook his head. "That's Fairlight for you, everyone wants to stare." He winked.

"Dad, you're not helping," Hannah sighed good-naturedly.

"Rosie will be so pleased to see you," Alice said. She looked around the playground and spotted the girl on the climbing frame with Simone.

"Has she grown yet?" Jon asked with a chuckle.

"Not much," Hannah admitted.

"It's the big brain, squishing down the rest of her body," Jon said. "I'm looking forward to babysitting her while I'm here. Will give you two some time alone."

Alice felt the instant blush on her cheeks. Of course she wanted some alone time with Hannah, but she didn't need Hannah's dad bringing it up.

"GRANDDAD!"

"She saw you, then," Hannah quipped.

Jon ran towards Rosie and scooped her up into a hug.

"Sorry about my dad, he likes to embarrass people," Hannah said.

"He's sweet," Alice admitted. "Certainly better than the reaction you would have gotten from my parents."

Hannah put a supportive arm around her shoulder.

Alice turned to talk to her when she noticed something out of the corner of her eye. Colin sat alone by the fence. She frowned.

Hannah followed her gaze.

"I'm going to go and talk to him," Alice said.

"Has he said much?" Hannah asked.

"No, he's kept to himself all day. It needs to be resolved. I'll catch you later."

"Okay, I'll see you for the assembly in an hour," Hannah said. "Don't worry, you'll be fine."

Alice didn't hear anything else as she was already walking toward Colin, noticing only now that he was crying. He may have been a troublesome little monster, but he was only five.

She silently sat on the ground beside him, grass stains be damned.

"What's wrong?" she asked.

"No one likes me." He wiped the tears away from his face with his sleeve.

"Why do you think that is?"

"Because they're stupid!" Colin spat out.

Alice sat quietly and waited.

"And… I'm mean to them," he confessed.

"Why do you do that?"

"I don't know." He shrugged.

Alice believed him. He was a little too young to understand his own behaviour.

"Maybe," she started, "you don't want people to hurt you. So you hurt them first?"

He thought about that for a few seconds and then nodded his head. "Maybe."

"Maybe I can help you with that?"

He turned and looked at her. "You should hate me, too. I nearly killed you and Rosie."

"I could never *hate* you, Colin. I want you to be happy. I want all of my students to be happy. And I think you'd be a lot happier if you made friends."

"They don't want to be friends."

"I think you'd be surprised." Alice stood and held out her hand to help him up. He stared for a few moments before grabbing it and pulling himself up. She rested a hand on his shoulder and looked around the playground.

A few boys from her class were playing football, and she nodded her head in their direction.

"Why don't you try and join in that game?"

He shook his head. "They hate me."

"You think everyone hates you," she chided. "Come on." She walked over to the football game, Colin falling into step behind her.

The boys stopped playing when she arrived.

"Boys, can Colin play with you?" she asked, gesturing him to come closer.

Peter shrugged. Quentin said, "Sure."

She bent down to Colin. "Just try to be nice. You'll be surprised. When you're nice, so are other people."

He nodded. She stood up and walked back towards Hannah.

"Did it go well?" Hannah asked.

"I think so. He's not a bad boy, just a little defensive. Like someone else I know. He gets the first punch in."

Hannah chuckled. "Smart kid."

Alice elbowed her playfully. She turned around and saw that Jon was now playing hopscotch with Rosie.

"So, your dad is happy to babysit Rosie?" Alice asked.

"Yeah, he's staying at a local bed and breakfast, and they have a spare room. He's stayed there before. Not sure how we'll fill the time," Hannah said casually.

"I have a couple of ideas," Alice replied, "but I'm not talking about them in a school playground."

The bell sounded to signal the end of break.

"What's the last lesson of the day?" Hannah asked.

"Maths."

"Last thing on a Monday? That's cruel!"

"Your daughter loves maths," Alice said.

"I'm going to order a DNA check," Hannah muttered.

"You do that. I'm going to go teach children valuable life skills," Alice said.

"I'm going to help set up the school hall for a hero," Hannah replied.

"Oh, shut up," Alice whispered so the passing children didn't hear her. "See you later."

Alice turned and followed the children towards the building. She noticed Colin was chatting animatedly with the boys she had left him with. She hoped some friendships were being formed. She knew she had a way to go with Colin. Behaviour didn't change overnight, not even after the shock of the fire, but he was making some good first steps.

37

ASSEMBLY

HANNAH LOOKED around the school hall. Everyone had turned up. She was pretty sure most of the shops in town had been closed so people could come to the school to see the assembly. Alice would hate it.

The mayor walked in, her large, gold chains of office clanking around her neck.

"They still know how to do overkill, then," Hannah's dad mumbled in her ear.

"Oh, yes," she agreed.

The bell sounded, thirty minutes earlier than the usual end of school, to give students time to get to the hall for the assembly to take place.

Children started to file in and take their seats on the wooden benches that had been set up for them. Parents, grandparents, staff, and everyone else from Fairlight stood around the perimeter of the room, waiting.

A photographer snapped pictures, and a few parents filmed proceedings.

Hannah couldn't blame them. Everyone was relieved that the fire hadn't been worse, that they were able to celebrate all being well rather than the alternative.

A few more classes entered the hall and took their seats.

Hannah remembered being in the school, sitting in the front of the hall in year one and slowly working her way through the benches until she sat at the back. And then, freedom. She'd never thought she'd be back.

The sound of children gasping and muttering caused her to look up. The fire service had arrived. They'd obviously always been considered heroes in the town, but they were now more so than ever. None of the officers would be able to buy themselves a drink in any of the local pubs for the next twelve months.

Finally, year one filed into the hall, and Alice guided them into their places. Hannah had to smile. It was a little like herding cats. She didn't know how Alice managed to cope with them all.

When they were all settled, Alice stood to the side, but not before finding Hannah and offering her a shy smile across the room.

Everyone was ready, the doors were closed, and Hardaker took to the stage.

"Thank you all for coming," he started. "As you all know, we're very lucky to sit in this hall with every single student and teacher with us. The fire started in the basement, due to faulty wiring. It could have started at any time, and we were very lucky it started at break time when the majority of people were out of the building.

"One young first-year student remained in the building, and if it weren't for the heroic act of Miss Spencer, she certainly wouldn't have survived."

Hannah felt a lump in her throat. Of course, she knew all this, but hearing it recapped in such a stark summary reminded her of how close she came to nearly losing Rosie. Her dad wrapped a strong arm around her shoulder and held her tight.

"We're very lucky that Miss Spencer reacted quickly to a deadly situation. And, as a symbol of our thanks, we have a plaque that will hang in the main entranceway. Miss Spencer, if you'd like to come up here?"

Alice walked up the small flight of steps onto the stage. The mayor walked up the other set of stairs holding a wooden plaque with an engraved brass sheet on it. They shook hands in the middle of the stage, and the plaque was handed from the mayor to Alice, with a few words exchanged.

"Speech!" Lucy Gibson shouted out from year two's section.

Alice shot her a dark look which just caused people to laugh. More calls for a speech sounded.

"And now," Hardaker said, "Miss Spencer will, apparently, say a few words."

Alice looked pleadingly at Hardaker. He held his hands up, indicating that it wasn't up to him.

Alice turned to face the audience. She looked down at the plaque for a few moments before looking up again. "When I came to Fairlight, I thought it would be just another job," she began. "But it didn't take me long to realise that Fairlight is much more than that. It's a community. I used to live in a large city, surrounded by thousands of people, but I'd never been more alone. Now, I feel like I've found a home."

She looked directly at Hannah. "And a family."

Alice broke eye contact. "I want to thank everyone who came together to get the school back up and running. Thank you to everyone who donated their time, expertise, or materials. And, of course, thank you to the paramedics, hospital staff, and the fire service, without whom, I wouldn't be here today."

Alice looked down at the front row of benches. "And, most of all, I'd like to say thank you to Rosie Hall for being so brave. I think we saved each other."

Everyone broke into applause. Hannah only realised a few tears had escaped when Mrs Palmer handed her a tissue.

"Thank you," Hannah whispered as she dabbed at her tears.

Alice posed with Hardaker, the fire officers, and the mayor for a few pictures on the stage, with her plaque in her hands. The other teachers guided the children out of the hall.

"She's something else."

Hannah looked at her dad. "She is."

"Maybe she's the one?" he pressed.

"It's really early yet," Hannah said, not wanting to have this conversation with her father.

"I've seen how you look at each other."

"Da-aad," she whined.

He held up his hands. "Okay, okay!" He looked across the room and grinned. "Is Mrs Harper still single?"

"She's still a miserable old battleaxe, so, yes, she's still single."

"Good. I'm going to work some of the Hall magic on her." He left, and Hannah felt a little queasy at the thought.

Alice approached and looked over at the couple. "Aw, sweet. She could be your new mum," she joked.

"That's not funny," Hannah complained, still feeling a little green.

Rosie appeared in front of them, looking serious as she often did when she'd had an idea and meant business. Hannah wondered if they were about to have yet another discussion about bedtime.

"I've been thinking about it," Rosie announced.

"Oh, yes?" Hannah asked.

"Yes. Miss Spencer's house is much bigger than ours," Rosie said.

They'd had lunch there the day before, not the sleepover Hannah desperately wanted, but they were on the way to getting Rosie comfortable enough in the unfamiliar surroundings.

"Yes, you're right," Hannah agreed, sharing a look with Alice as they both wondered what this was leading up to.

"And it has two bedrooms," Rosie carried on. "I think it would be nice if Mummy had her own bedroom, and then I could share with Miss Spencer. Or Mummy could share with Miss Spencer, and I can still have my own room. It makes more sense because Miss Spencer is always over at our house anyway."

Hannah wanted a hole to open up and suck her into its murky depths. Her daughter had basically invited them both to move in with her girlfriend. Her girlfriend, whom she had fallen in love with, but had only been seeing for a short period of time.

"That sounds like a great idea," Alice said.

Hannah snapped her head up and looked at Alice in surprise.

"It does?" she asked.

"I think so," Alice said. "What do you think? Would you be open to sharing a room with me?"

Hannah looked down at Rosie's eager face and then up to Alice's wide smile. "I… yes, I'd like that, I'd like that a lot."

"Well, then, we'll try it out one day and see what happens." Alice turned to Rosie. "What a wonderful idea. Thank you, Rosie."

Rosie beamed with pride before leaving to seek out her grandfather.

Hannah turned to Alice. "I'm so sorry, she doesn't know when to—"

"Hannah?" Alice interrupted.

"Yes?"

"I love you," Alice said simply. "Let's try being a family."

Hannah's mouth felt dry. Her heart hammered against her chest. Everything told her that it was too soon, but it also felt so right. Time away from Alice now felt like time wasted.

She wanted to spend every moment with her.

"I'd love that," she admitted. She cupped Alice's face and leaned in to kiss her.

Whoops sounded from the still-crowded room, and Hannah pulled back and laughed, blushing as she did.

"Let's get out of here," she whispered.

THE END

PATREON

I adore publishing. There's a wonderful thrill that comes from crafting a manuscript and then releasing it to the world. Especially when you are writing woman loving woman characters. I'm blessed to receive messages from readers all over the world who are thrilled to discover characters and scenarios that resemble their lives.

Books are entertaining escapism, but they are also reinforcement that we are not alone in our struggles. I'm passionate about writing books that people can identify with. Books that are accessible to all and show that love—and acceptance—can be found no matter who you are.

I've been lucky enough to have published books that have been best-sellers and even some award-winners. While I'm still quite a new author, I have plans to write many, many more novels. However, writing, editing, and marketing books take up a lot of time... and writing full-time is a treadmill-like existence, especially in a very small niche market like mine.

Don't get me wrong, I feel very grateful and lucky to

be able to live the life I do. But being a full-time author in a small market means never being able to stop and work on developing my writing style, it means rarely having the time or budget to properly market my books, it means immediately picking up the next project the moment the previous has finished.

This is why I have set up a Patreon account. With Patreon, you can donate a small amount each month to enable me to hop off of my treadmill for a while in order to reach my goals. Goals such as exploring better marketing options, developing my writing craft, and investigating writing articles and screenplays.

My Patreon page is a place for exclusive first looks at new works, insight into upcoming projects, Q&A sessions, as well as special gifts and dedications. I'm also pleased to give all of my Patreon subscribers access to **exclusive short stories** which have been written just for patrons. There are tiers to suit all budgets.

My readers are some of the kindest and most supportive people I have met, and I appreciate every book borrow or purchase. With the added support of Patreon, I hope to be able to develop my writing career in order to become a better author as well as level up my marketing strategy to help my books to reach a wider audience.

https://www.patreon.com/aeradley

REVIEWS

I sincerely hope you enjoyed reading this book.

If you did, I would greatly appreciate a short review on your favourite book website.

Reviews are crucial for any author, and even just a line or two can make a huge difference.

ABOUT THE AUTHOR

Amanda Radley had no desire to be a writer but accidentally became an award-winning, bestselling author.

She gave up a marketing career in order to make stuff up for a living instead. She claims the similarities are startling.

She describes herself as a Wife. Traveller. Tea Drinker. Biscuit Eater. Animal Lover. Master Pragmatist. Procrastinator. Theme Park Fan.

Connect with Amanda
www.amandaradley.com

FITTING IN

2020 Amazon Kindle Storyteller Finalist

Starting a new job is hard. Especially if you're the boss's daughter

Heather Bailey has been in charge of Silver Arches, the prestigious London shopping centre, for several years. Financial turmoil brings a new investor to secure the future and Heather finds herself playing office politics with the notoriously difficult entrepreneur Leo Flynn. Walking a fine line between standing her ground and being willing to accept change, Heather has her work cut out for her.

When Leo demands that his daughter is found a job at Silver Arches; things become even harder.

Scarlett Flynn has never fit in. Not in the army, not in her father's firm, not even in her own family. So starting work at Silver Arches won't be any different, will it?

A heartwarming exploration of the art of fitting in.

GOING UP

2020 Selfies Finalist

A ruthless executive. A destitute woman. Both on the way up.

Selina Hale is on her way to the top. She's been working towards a boardroom position on the thirteenth floor for her entire career. And no one is going to get in her way. Not her clueless boss, her soon to be ex-wife, and most certainly not the homeless person who has moved into the car park at work.

Kate Morgan fell through the cracks in a broken support system and found herself destitute. Determined and strong-willed, she's not about to accept help from a mean business woman who can't even remember the names of her own nephews.

As their lives continue to intertwine, they have no choice but to work together and follow each other on their journey up.

LOST AT SEA

A stowaway. A perceptive captain. Both drawn together.

Annie Peck finds herself in a terrible situation and is literally running for her life. A chance encounter with a surprising lookalike leads her towards a risky solution.

Captain Caroline West knows she is lucky to be one of the few women cruise ship captains in the world. Sadly, not having a standard nine to five job means relationships are nearly impossible and she's all but given up on finding anyone.

Join these two women for an all-expenses-paid cruise of the Mediterranean and find out what happens when an identity thief with a heart of gold meets the rule-abiding woman who could throw her in jail.

www.ingramcontent.com/pod-product-compliance
Lightning Source LLC
Chambersburg PA
CBHW021201250626
47155CB00008B/2624